秦始皇帝

YING ZHENG
THE FIRST EMPEROR

A Novel

David Johnson

Strategic Book Publishing and Rights Co.

Copyright © 2013

All rights reserved – David Johnson

No part of this book may be reproduced or transmitted in any form or by any means, graphic, electronic, or mechanical, including photocopying, recording, taping, or by any information storage retrieval system, without the permission, in writing, from the publisher.

Strategic Book Publishing and Rights Co.
12620 FM 1960, Suite A4-507
Houston, TX 77065
www.sbpra.com

ISBN: 978-1-62212-289-9

It would have been very difficult to tell this story without the consistent encouragement of my sister, Terrie Jo Wold, and her husband, the Reverend Steven Wold.

CONTENTS

Introduction ... vii

Part I—Lu Buwei

Chapter 1	1
Chapter 2	11
Chapter 3	27
Chapter 4	39
Chapter 5	57
Chapter 6	63
Chapter 7	73
Chapter 8	85

Part II—Conquest

Chapter 9	91
Chapter 10	101
Chapter 11	113
Chapter 12	125

Part III—Emperor

Chapter 13	137
Chapter 14	147
Chapter 15	157
Chapter 16	171
Afterword	183
Bibliography	187

INTRODUCTION

If I were to tell most readers that I want to tell a story about Qin Shi Huangdi I would be met with blank expressions. If, on the other hand, I were say that the story would be about the emperor that conquered all of China; built the terra-cotta army and a huge unopened mysterious mausoleum; built the Great Wall of China by working thousands of people to their deaths; burned the books of Confucius and buried hundreds of Confucian scholars alive; built a huge number of palaces and then secretly moved from one to another to avoid assassination attempts; and spent his life looking for the "elixir of life," the reader would say "Oh, that guy!" This character has appeared in movies, books, television shows, and video games including *Indiana Jones and the Emperor's Tomb*, *Civilization IV*, *Tomb Raider Lara Croft*, and others.

The Qin emperor left a long legacy, which can be seen in an infamous quote by Mao Zedong. After being criticized for his treatment of intellectuals, the chairman said, "He buried 460 scholars alive, we have buried 46,000 scholars alive … You (intellectuals) revile us for being Qin Shi Huangs. You are wrong. We have surpassed Qin Shi Huang a hundredfold."

Most of what we know of Qin Shi Huangdi comes from the *Records of the Grand Historian*, written by Sima Qian during the succeeding Han Dynasty. We often forget that the modern idea of history is very different from that which existed in the past. Ancient histories are usually better described as "story telling," and in the case of Sima Qian's masterpiece, some of the tales approach tabloid sensationalism.

It was very popular to vilify the emperor in the Han Dynasty. The Confucians compiled a list of "Ten Crimes of Qin," and the poet Jia Yi wrote an essay entitled "The Faults of Qin." The *Records of the Grand Historian* certainly fit into this genre. In modern times, a revisionist version has arisen, with some calling the emperor "…one of the great heroes of Chinese history." The truth is certainly somewhere in-between.

It is not my intention to find this "truth." I am telling a story. That story will seek to explore possible realities behind some of the more sensational tales but it is still just a story.

Qin Shi Huangdi was born with the name Ying Zheng. The story begins with his tenth year; thus, our timeframe is from 249 to 210 B.C.

Warring States 250 B.C.

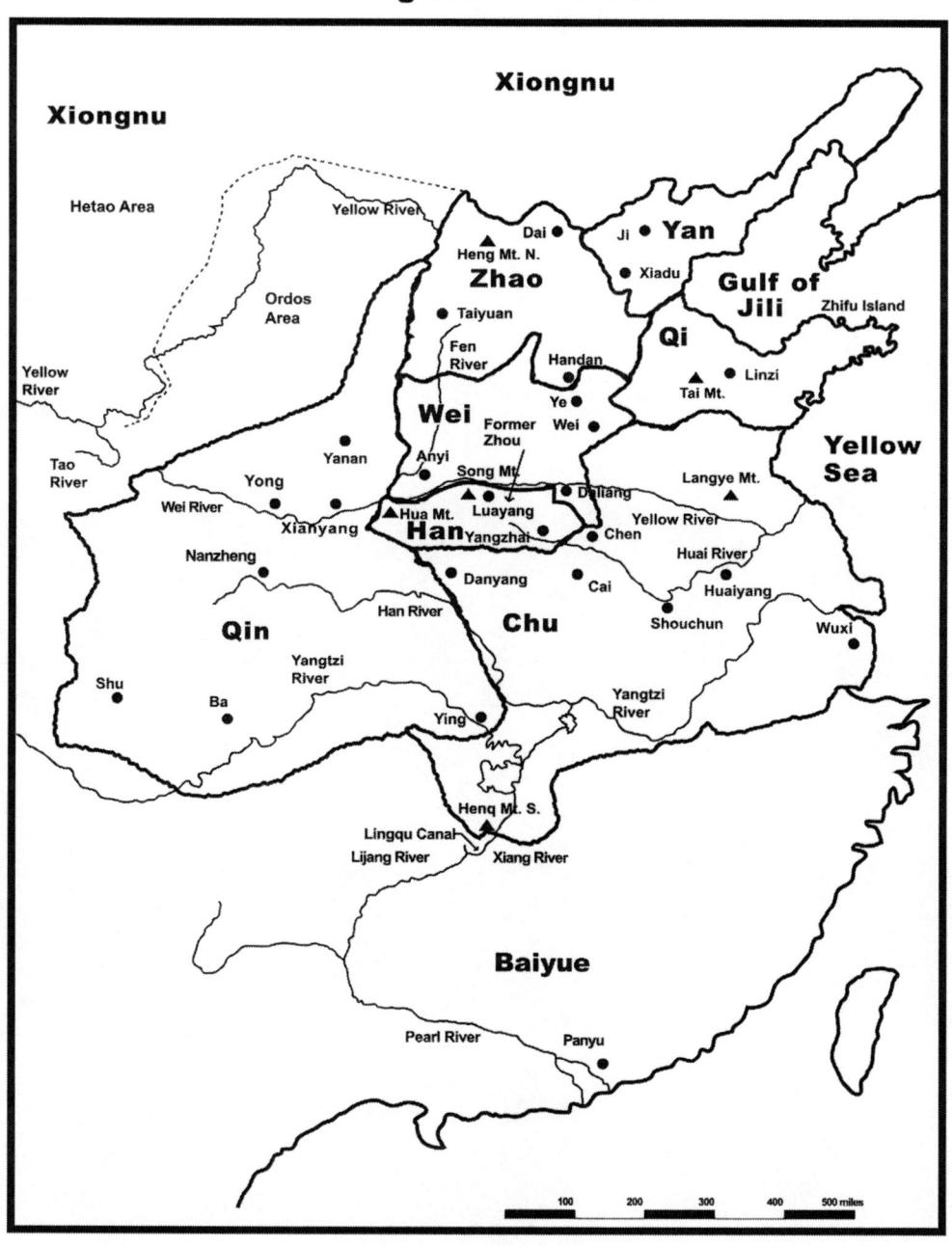

PART I
Lu Buwei

CHAPTER 1

It was a bright and warm summer afternoon in Handan, the capital city of Zhao. Lu Buwei and Ying Yiren were having tea on the porch of an elegant residence in the palace complex. Lu Buwei had just returned from a year-long business trip. The two men were quite different in appearance. The thirty-five-year-old Ying Yiren was tall and slender. Lu Buwei was ten years older and shorter. He combined a strong body with bulky shoulders and arms with a good-sized belly that came from a love of exotic food. He had twinkling eyes and a gregarious manner that was easy to like. Ying Yiren, by contrast, had a face that reflected a hard past and the stoic acceptance of a future with little promise.

Ying Yiren's ten-year-old son was playing in the small garden that fronted the house. Beyond him was a well-groomed road with colorful buildings on each side. In the distance was the great palace of King Dan. Lu Buwei spoke: "Have you been well?"

"Yes, Master."

Lu Buwei smiled. He was not a master of anything. He described himself as a "humble merchant," although many people knew that he was much more than that. Buwei did indeed conduct trade. His business in Zhao was the acquisition of fine bronzeware, which his "associates" turned into profit by trade in other states. This was, however, only part of his business. Lu Buwei provided services. If you desired a beautiful concubine from a distant land, Buwei could provide one. If you desired a rare object, Buwei could deliver it. And, if you were an aristocrat in need of a large loan, Lu Buwei was available. His interest rates were modest, but the borrower knew that no matter how high the position or the more lofty the title, it did not excuse payment.

Still he liked his young guest's expression of respect. Ying Yiren and his family had lived with him for ten years. He was fond of them while remembering that they were an opportunity to be carefully guarded.

"And your mother, Lady Xia?"

"She is well."

"And the lovely Lady Zhao?"

"Again well."

Lady Zhao had been Lu Buwei's concubine and he had given her to Ying Yiren when the young man was brought to his house. They soon had a son—the same child now playing in the garden.

"Is little Ying Zheng keeping up with his studies?"

"Indeed, Master—he is doing quite well. I must thank you again for providing such a wise teacher."

"You are, of course, welcome. Let's test the young man."

Ying Yiren called for his son, and the youth joined them. Lu Buwei began his examination: "Why was the Yellow Emperor yellow?"

"Because, Uncle, he was the first of the five divine kings that ruled Man in antiquity; and the first of the five elements is earth. Earth's color is yellow."

"And who founded the next dynasty?"

"The last of the five divine kings was Shun. He chose Yu Hsiahou for his great merit and work taming the rivers. Emperor Yu was the great-great-grandson of the Yellow Emperor, Huangdi Yuhsiung. His dynasty was called 'Xia.' As the second dynasty, it was represented by the second element, wood, whose color is green."

"Why is wood the second element?"

"Wood overcomes earth by division."

"Excellent. Now what followed the dynasty of Xia?"

"The Emperor Tang overthrew the tyrant Chieh and founded the dynasty named 'Shang.' As the third dynasty, it was represented by the third element, metal, whose color is white."

"Why is metal the third element?"

"Because, Uncle, metal overcomes wood by cutting it."

"Now I see the color red on banners and robes when I am traveling in the state of Zhou. Why is that?"

"The Zhou dynasty was the last dynasty. It was the fourth and the fourth element is fire—whose color is red."

"Again, why is fire the fourth element?"

"Fire overcomes metal by melting it."

"Today we have no emperor. The land is divided into many states. What if we see another dynasty that unites the people? Will it have a color?"

"Yes. The fifth element is water—whose color is black. Water overcomes fire by quenching."

"Good. You know history. Now a more important subject—name the nine virtues."

"In truth, Uncle, there are eighteen. These are arranged in pairs to make nine. They are: liberality and dignity, mildness and firmness, bluntness and respect, aptness and caution, docility and boldness, straightforwardness and gentleness, easy negligence and discrimination, resolution and sincerity, courage and justice.

"These are the nine virtues."

"Excellent. You may return to your play."

Ying Zhen ran off and was soon joined by another boy of about the same age. They sat in the garden, engaged in some sort of game.

Turing to Ying Yiren, Lu Buwei said, "Your son has done well. He has clearly paid attention to his studies. Has he read the classics?"

"Yes, Master. In fact, we are reading them together."

"And who is his companion?"

"He is another hostage being held here. You can see his guards posted over there." Ying Yiren pointed to three nearby soldiers who were talking among themselves while keeping an eye on their charge. He continued: "His name is Dan. He is the son of King Xi of Yan. He and Zheng have become good friends."

Lu Buwei was silent and mused while he sipped his tea. It was important, even with a guest, to avoid coming directly to the point. After a few minutes, he continued: "Ying Yiren, do you ever think of Qin?"

"Not very much. As you know, my mother and I were sent here as hostages by my grandfather, King Ying Ze, to secure peace following the defeat of two Qin armies by the Zhao's General Lian Po.

I was twelve years old. That was a long time ago."

"And that time was hard for both of you."

"Yes. We were assigned to a small house here on the palace grounds. We were guarded around the clock and could not leave the house. We shared a single bed and our food, such as it was, was delivered. For years the only thing we ate was coarse rice and an occasional weak soup."

"And for all of that it took Zhao only six years before they broke the peace."

"Yes, and the decision turned out to be unfortunate for Zhao," Ying Yiren said.

"There has never been such a battle. Zhao accepted a request for help from the state of Han, and its army met the army of Qin at Changping. The battle was started by General Lian Po against the Qin General Weng He. The conflict lasted three years, and both sides replaced their generals. Zhao sent General Zhao Kuo and Qin set General Bai Qi. I am told that 400,000 men from Zhao died. General Bai Qi not only killed men in combat but he also buried survivors alive. It was a shock to the entire state."

"The tactics of General Bai Qi during the final engagement will be studied for many years."

"I am sure that is true," Lu Buwei said. "But that is not the point in regard to the current conversation. This huge defeat was followed by a siege of Handan. Zhao only survived because the state of Wei came to its aid. In the aftermath of these events, King Dan did not know what to do with the two of you. Thankfully he was a good friend, although a rather expensive one. When I asked to take you, he accepted readily."

Lu Buwei strengthened his "business" by giving gifts to important people. The king of each state was always one of the primary recipients. King Dan had received many exotic gifts from distant lands. It was because of these gifts that Lu Buwei was granted his fine house and was left alone to conduct his affairs.

"I have just returned from Qin. Your grandfather King Ying Ze has died after ruling for fifty-six years. He is to be remembered as 'Zhaoxiang.' I am told that your father, Lord Anguo, intends to take the throne. He has already selected his throne name. He is to be known as 'Xiaowen.'"

"My mother will not like to hear this news," Ying Yiren said. "It is true that we are here at the command of my grandfather, but it was my father who made the selection. She carries a good deal of resentment for that decision."

"Well, she must exercise patience. I spoke with Lord Anguo's favorite concubine, and while the lord is against your return, I think she will support you in the right circumstances."

"And who is this woman?"

"She is called Lady Huayang."

* * *

Over the next few weeks, Ying Yiren observed small groups of men come to Buwei's house. They would stay awhile and then leave, their meetings always private. In itself, this was not unusual. There were always "associates" coming for meetings. Now, however, the frequency of these meetings was much higher—at times almost daily. One time, as he was passing in a corridor, he heard a few words. "Yes. But there are men who would do this, and accept their fate, if it meant that their families would be taken care of."

"But do such men have the required skill?"

Ying Yiren continued on at a faster pace. The words were mysterious and could be dangerous, but without knowing the context it was hard to make a judgment. It was probably innocent. Lu Buwei was a businessman, and businessmen were only interested in profit.

After the series of visitors, Lu Buwei announced that he was going to the city of Wei to visit his father.

* * *

The cities of Handan and Wei are relatively close and the journey only required a few days. Lu Buwei arrived in the late afternoon to a warm welcome. After a pleasant supper, he sat with his father. They talked about many things, then Lu brought up his main thought: "Father, what is the profit on investment that one can expect from plowing fields?"

"Ten times the investment."

"And the return on investment in pearls and jades is how much?"

"A hundredfold"

"And the return on investment from establishing a ruler and securing the state would be how much?"

"It would be incalculable."

"Now if I devoted my energies to laboring in the fields, I would hardly get enough to clothe and feed myself; yet if I secure a state and establish its lord, the benefits can be passed on to future generations. I propose to go serve Prince Yiren of Qin, who is hostage in Zhao."

Lu Buwei spent the night and began his return to Handan early, at first light.

*　*　*

Buwei arrived home late. After a private breakfast in his rooms, he asked Ying Yiren to join him on the porch for tea. As was the custom, the two men sat silently for few minutes. Lu Buwei spoke first: "I have a question, and I need a truthful answer."

He paused, then continued: "Are you happy here?"

"Master, you have been extremely kind to my family. You have provided the best food, fine clothing of silk and jewelry for my mother and wife, teachers for my son—and, most of all, security in a hostile city. How could I not be happy?"

"I repeat, are you happy here?"

Ying Yiren was silent for a long time. Finally he said, "Well … I am still a prisoner. Yes, a prisoner in a comfortable prison. I have been treated well, but I have nothing to do. The idleness and isolation are suffocating. So I guess I could truthfully say that I am less than happy."

"Very good. Now, what if I could make you a king?"

"You can do that?"

"I believe so, but you must stop calling me 'Master.'"

Lu Buwei again waited in silence. He watched his companion's face and saw a glimmer of hope gradually appear for brief moment, only to be replaced by confusion.

"But Mas—excuse me … how can this happen?"

"A number of significant events will occur in the next few weeks. When they happen, we need to be on the road to Qin. It is a very long journey and we need to start very soon. It will mean that we must leave Lady Xia, Lady Zhao, and Ying Zheng here. I have made arrangements for their security and comfort. In due time, they can join us."

"But I am still a prisoner."

"That has also been arranged. The gate guards have been paid well. By the time anyone else notices, we will be far enough away. I suspect that King Dan will be relieved by your escape."

"How soon do we have to leave?"

"Tomorrow morning. Pack a few things. You will not need much. We can buy what is necessary on the way. Say your goodbyes tonight. Tell your family that you are traveling with me on a trade mission. Once we are well on the way, I can tell you more. For now you must trust me and do everything I tell you to do."

* * *

Lu Buwei and Ying Yiren had been traveling in their cart for two weeks. The capital of Qin, Xianyang, was getting closer. The horses had been changed a few times and were holding up well with the easy pace Buwei had set. The men had talked of a number of things during the journey but Buwei was still quiet regarding their mission. Now Lu Buwei thought the time had come. "Ying Yiren, in one week's time, the events that I spoke of will take place. Your father will die. So will Duke Wugong, of Zhou."

Buwei saw Ying Yiren's eyes widened in surprise. He continued: "And you will have a new mother."

Ying Yiren turned pale in shock. He responded with difficulty. "How—why?"

"I do not know how these two worthies will die, but they will die nonetheless. As to why, the demise of Duke Wugong is a business matter. As to King Xiaowen, the reason is simple enough: you can only occupy a throne that is empty."

"I mean … I don't understand. Why do I have to have a new mother?"

"Well, your father had many concubines and he was very busy. He has a total of twenty sons. His favorite concubine is Lady Huayang. She is, however, childless. As favorite, she has privilege and rank. With a son of her own, she can decide the succession. She will adopt you and give you a new name. You will then become King of Qin. It is a solution that will be appealing for many. There are few things that can weaken a state more than a disputed succession. Qin has already suffered one such ordeal in the past and does not want another. As to Lady Huayang, she desires to be Queen Dowager. With you as king, that position is hers."

The cold-blooded ruthless logic of it all was frightening. Ying Yiren was being plunged into the icy waters of politics.

CHAPTER 2

At the Xianyang palace complex, Lu Buwei and Ying Yiren were met by guards who inquired of their business. When they said they needed to see Lady Huayang, they were detained until permission was received. They were escorted by six guards to one of the residence buildings and were held outside her apartment until announced.

They entered the reception room with the guards. The guards remained until Lady Huayang dismissed them, but they only retired to the room's entrance. They closed the doors and the three were alone. Lady Huayang was rather tall. She wore a beautiful silk robe with wide shoulder supports. Her eyes were piercing and were framed by long, coal black hair that was completely undone. She wore neither headpiece nor jewelry. While her face showed age, her posture and movements were that of a younger woman. She walked forward, her eyes fixed on Ying Yiren. She slowly circled and inspected him from head to toe.

"So, Lu Buwei, this is your forgotten prince?"

"Yes, Lady"

"Well, he has some of his father's features." She paused for what seemed to Yiren to be an eternity, then continued: "So … Ying Yiren … are you prepared to be a king?"

"No, Majesty."

"Well, you do not have much time." Turning to Lu Buwei she said with a measured tone: "King Xiaowen died yesterday. I suppose that you had nothing to do with that. Or did you?"

Buwei feigned surprise. Yiren did not have to. He was shocked by the fulfillment of Buwei's prophecy. He did not want to believe what Buwei had told him. Now being confronted with reality he was filled with ambivalence that ranged from wonder to fear.

Lu Buwei replied, "Lady, we were on the road to your city yesterday! How did this happen?"

"The physician called it heart failure, and I suppose that was right—his heart was beating before, and it wasn't afterward. Personally, I suspect poison. All I know is that whoever did this left us with two vacancies in the government. Lord Anguo was chancellor and had not selected a replacement."

Turning to Ying Yiren, she said, "So, young man, if you become king, you will need to name a replacement chancellor. And if you become king, I will be Queen Dowager. Do you know what that means?"

"No, Majesty"

"It means I can overrule any decision that you make—and I am not 'Majesty' yet, young man."

Lady Huayang walked across the room and sat on a woven bamboo mat. Addressing both men, she continued: "The only people who know of the king's death are the physician, the Commandant of Guards and those guards that he has assigned to the king's quarters. I have assured them that if the news comes out before I decide, both the offender and his superior will be executed. Now that same sentence applies to both of you."

Turning again to Ying Yiren, she said, "Now, we need to name you. I come from the State of Chu. Therefore, I have decided to name you 'Zichu.' You may keep your family name, 'Ying.' It connects you to the royal line. From this moment on you are my son and I am your mother. The Lord Secretary will prepare and issue an edict to that effect. That will be followed by an edict naming you as the designated Crown Prince to King Xiaowen. I should tell you now that the Lord Secretary is your older half-brother, Ying Changjio, now known as Lord Changan. If there is serious opposition, it will probably come from him.

"Your first official act, before the public announcement of the death of King Xiaowen, will be to call a private court session. This will be attended by Lord Changan, Grand Commandant Lord Biao, the ministers, and a few others. You will ask this group to recommend your throne name. If they do in fact deliberate, it will be a sign that you have been accepted by the government—for now. I will be present and I will announce the passing of the king. The palace guard will be stationed in an adjoining room. At this time you may also announce the name of the future chancellor. Do you have a candidate in mind?"

"Yes, Lady Huayang, I would like to name my friend, protector, and council Lu Buwei."

"I expected as much," she said, then. "So, Lu Buwei, if Zichu knows nothing of being a king, how much do you know about being a Qin chancellor?"

"Alas, Lady, nothing"

"Well, we will have to see about instruction. At least I know that you are highly skilled in politics, and advice on that subject will be valuable to our new king." She waved her hand. "Now, leave me. Tell the guard that you are to be provided quarters."

* * *

That evening Lu Buwei left the palace grounds and entered the city. Surrounding the palace gates were a number of large houses. They had once been grand but were now in decline. The families who lived there were also in decline. They were the descendants of the proud nobles who had ruled the fiefdoms of Qin. The hated Shang Yang took their domains a century earlier and gave the land to the people. In the time of King Huiwen, Lord Shang had been torn apart by chariots. Ever since, the families had waited in the hope that the old system would return. After all, other states found that fiefdoms worked. Surely Qin would come to its senses. Only it never happened. They were left with their pride and dwindling resources with no chance of a better life elsewhere.

For Lu Buwei's partner, Li Ziyan, it was an opportunity. He found in these families a ready source of fine objects both contemporary and ancient. These could be traded for substantial profit. His best customers were, like Lu Buwei's, in distant states. Other merchants had their own specialties, and together they formed a silent informal government without boundaries. It was to Li Ziyan's house that Lu Buwei was now walking.

Li Ziyan welcomed him warmly. He ordered tea, and they moved to a small room at the rear of the house that was comfortably furnished with two mats and a beautifully decorated table. Lu Buwei settled his bulk on one mat and Li Ziyan took its twin.

"This is most welcome, Buwei. You have not visited my house for a long time,, and now I have had the pleasure of two visits in a matter of months."

"You are most welcome, my friend."

"Buwei, you must send me more of your fine bronzes. The palace nobles and officials have developed quite an appetite for them."

"I will gladly arrange a shipment."

The tea was brought in and they were left alone. They sipped their tea quietly for a time. Then Li Ziyan spoke: "Were the arrangements to your satisfaction?"

"Yes. The matter was completed most satisfactorily. I would like to ask another favor."

"Certainly"

"Li Ziyan, I have decided to enter into the business of government."

"That is a worthy challenge. How can I help?"

"I have not spent much time learning this craft, and I understand that the government of Qin is unusual in some of its aspects."

"That is quite true."

"Could you please describe their system?"

"Gladly. Qin uses a system called 'Three Lords and Nine Ministers.' The three lords are the Grand Commandant, the Lord Secretary, and the Chancellor. Currently the Chancellery is vacant."

"Yes. This is the position I intend to occupy."

"Congratulations. Well, then let me concentrate on that office."

"That would be most helpful," Lu Buwei said.

"The chancellor has many duties and, like the other two lords, he has three ministers to help him complete those tasks. Together, the three ministers supervise nine departments.

"The Minister of the Palace manages the Commandant of Guards, the Grand Herald, and the Supervisor of Coachmen.

"The Minister of the Royal Family manages the Supervisor of Attendants, the Supervisor of Ceremonies, and the Supervisor of the Royal Clan.

"The Minister of State manages the Commandant of Justice, the Director of Agriculture, and the Treasurer.

"The chancellor, meanwhile, handles provincial reports, registry of land and population, maps, government budget and finances, and logistics for military campaigns. It is a very powerful position, but one that is held under very close accountability."

"How?"

"The three lords are considered to be absolutely equal in all respects—and that is the strength of the system. Now the Lord Secretary does those things that you expect a secretary to do: he has censorial powers over all reporting; he has the sole authority to issue edicts and other correspondence; he supervises the grand recorder; and he manages the Royal Library. These duties are not, however, his principle responsibility. The Lord Secretary is charged to prevent the abuse of authority and to uphold disciplinary procedures for ministers, officials, and all other members of government. He has a separate ministry to accomplish this task—the Ministry of Governmental Affairs. There is not a corner in the entire government that is not under its eye."

Lu Buwei considered all this and said, "This is clearly a man I would be wise to befriend."

"Yes. Now to this must be added the Grand Commandant. Lord Biao has three ministers: the Chief of Staff, the Minister of Strategic Planning, and the Minister of National Espionage. Of these, the Minister of National Espionage has a great deal of interest in both the army and the government. He looks for any signs of spies and corrupted officials who may be providing information to other states."

When Li Ziyan finished, they sat in silence for nearly an hour. Both men sipped their tea. Finally Lu Buwei broke the silence. "This is a very dangerous situation. I could be ruined by a single fool. I will need to have better knowledge than anyone else. Ziyan, you are wise as always, and your council valued. Could you have someone detail for me the names of the persons in these positions, and any other information that may be useful?"

"It will be done. It shall appear as a report from your own department, and sensitive material will be coded as appropriate."

"Thank you, my friend."

* * *

The first edict was issued the next day. The son of the king, Ying Zichu, was celebrated as the hostage who offered his life in the defense of Qin and survived the cruelty of Zhao. So great were his achievements that the king's favorite, Lady Huayang, had adopted him. On the following day, an edict was issued that proclaimed that King Xiaowen had named the hero, Ying Zichu as Crown Prince.

Lu Buwei told Zichu that the edicts indicated that Lord Changan had accepted Zichu for the time being. Privately he understood completely. It was often better to be the power behind the throne.

Exactly one week later, Lord Changan issued an order to Lord Biao and the ministers for an emergency council. The reason was secret to everyone, including the Lord Secretary.

On the day before the council, Lady Huayang took Ying Zichu with her as she attended the dead king. Xiaowen was surrounded by a huge quantity of flowers. Lady Huayang carefully inspected each blossom and replaced each spent flower with a fresh one. It was not a gesture of love or sorrow—it was strictly pragmatic. The body was beginning to smell.

Following this, Lady Huayang walked with her son across the broad courtyard to the palace. "Always be familiar with the terrain before accepting battle," she explained.

"A battle?"

"Oh yes. Tomorrow will be a battle—a political battle, but a battle nonetheless. You must treat it as such. You must exhibit the same courage and leadership as if you were leading an army against a powerful enemy. Keep everything to the point. Idle conversation will betray weakness."

The palace was of modest size, appearing more like a large temple than a center of government. There was an enclosed passage connecting it to the residence building. This was guarded and reserved for the king and those he might choose. The palace was constructed in the classical style and was both elegant and colorful. The building was elevated, and the only approach was a broad set of seven steps on the front side. It was surrounded on all four sides by red columns supporting a wide roof with earth-colored tiles. The building walls were black and decorated with wood panels that were carved in high relief with images that celebrated the history and traditions of Qin. These included the clan founder, the legendary Zhuanxu, who was one of the five divine kings. Also included was an ancestral head of the clan of Qin, Dafei, who was granted the family name "Ying" by the Emperor Yu—great-great-grandson of the Yellow Emperor and the father of the dynasty of Xia. The window frames and column tops were all colored yellow. Ying Zichu had seen the palace many times in his youth but had never seen the inside. Now the Lady Huayang was leading him up the steps to that magical place.

The double doors were opened by guards and they entered the reception room. Another set of double doors were opened by a second pair of guards and they entered the throne room. This room was large with a white tile floor and plain white walls and ceiling, and was punctuated by two rows of broad green columns, colored at their tops and bases with yellow.

The color scheme was just what Zichu had expected. In fact, it could be nothing else. The palace colors represented the yin and yang of opposing seasons. The red and black exterior corresponded to summer and winter. The green and white interior corresponded to spring and autumn. The color yellow was used for the intercalary period between summer and autumn when the difference between the solar and lunar cycles was adjusted.

At the rear of the room was a seven–foot-square platform elevated approximately one foot. The platform was covered with a richly decorated seating mat. Twenty-six smaller bamboo mats were placed twelve on each side of the room and one on each side of the platform. Each mat had a low rectangular table placed in front of it. On the back wall, centered on the platform, was a large embroidered screen. The center of this screen bore the image of a yellow dragon inside a four-colored circle of red, green, white, and black. On either side of the yellow dragon were a large fu symbol and the image of an axe head. At the top of the screen were a red bird and a black tortoise on circles of yellow. At the bottom were a green dragon and a white tiger, also in yellow circles. The fu symbol represented the ability to determine right from wrong. The axe head represented the power of decision. The remaining symbols represented the five elements, seasons, and divine creatures.

Ying Zichu explored the place. Behind the throne room was a slightly smaller room that was still of considerable size. It had a door at the rear that undoubtedly connected with the king's passage. It was here, he thought, that the palace guard would be placed. On each side of the throne room were long narrow compartments that were comfortably furnished with mats and tables. Outside windows illuminated the side and rear rooms while a skylight illuminated the throne room.

Standing by the platform, Ying Zichu asked, "So is this our battleground?"

"Yes, and this will be our strategy: you and I will wait in one of the side corridors until all the lords and ministers are present. We will wait until they are slightly uncomfortable, and then we will enter. They will remain standing until the king is seated—which, of course, will not happen. You will stand in front of the mat on the right of the king's mat, and I will stand in front of the one on the left. I will announce the death of the king and then defer to you. Address the group on your feet."

* * *

The day of the court session arrived. Lady Huayang and Ying Zichu arrived early and waited as planned. Lady Huayang appeared very different than on their first meeting. Her hair was bound, and she wore a magnificent head piece. Her silk gown was similar, but more elaborate and colorful. She wore jewelry on both arms, along with rings and a necklace. Makeup with red emphasized lips, and drawn eyebrows completed the presentation. She looked like she already was the Queen Dowager.

A guard informed them when all were present. Lady Huayang turned and spoke to Zichu: "I understand that you have a concubine and a son in Handan."

"A *wife* and son; I also have a mother."

"I know. After this is over, you must send for them. Lady Zhao and Ying Zheng will be extremely welcome at court. I am uncertain on the best course for Lady Xia. I do, however, promise that she will be treated extremely well and you will be able to spend time with her."

"Is she to be exiled or imprisoned?"

"Of course not. This is a matter that can be solved to everyone's satisfaction. But it does require that Lady Xia and I have a conversation."

The two sat silently for a few more moments, then Lady Huayang announced, "It is time. I will enter first, and you will follow."

Lady Huayang entered the room and remained standing in her position until Ying Zichu had found his. There were twenty men standing in front of them with mixed expressions. All were dressed in their finest official robes, hats, and jewels. Lord Biao wore full armor with a silk cape. Lady Huayang paused for a few more moments, and then announced in a grave voice: "I regret to inform you that our King Xiaowen has died. I have been assured by the physician that the cause was heart failure."

There was a storm of conversation between the men present. This was incorrect protocol, but it was excusable as this was a private session. When they finally quieted, Lord Changan asked the question for all of them: "Is the Crown Prince to assume the throne?"

"It is my hope that he will. He is standing there. There are, however, more pressing issues. There must be a formal announcement of this sad event, to be followed by a burial with appropriate ceremony and prayers to King Xiaowen and his ancestors. As to the Crown Prince, it is not my place to ask him to accept this duty."

Again there was a storm of conversation, and again quiet followed, with Lord Changan speaking for all: "The Minister of Ceremonies will arrange everything required. We will all provide him any assistance needed. I will draft the announcement but we need a head of state. Prince Ying Zichu will you accept the throne of Qin?"

Ying Zichu replied, "Yes, but I have two requirements."

"Please state them, Your Majesty."

"First, I want you all to agree to serve me and the state of Qin. This is not a time for change. Second, I would like you to recommend my throne name."

Looks were exchanged all around. Several ministers were seen nodding assent. Lord Changan replied, "We would be proud to meet these terms. May we confer immediately?"

"Yes. Lady Huayang and I will retire to the waiting chamber. Please announce when you are ready."

They returned to the room where they waited before. Neither spoke. An hour passed, and then Lord Changan knocked softly on the door.

"Your Majesty, we have made a choice."

Both returned to the courtroom, and Lord Changan continued: "Your Majesty, we want to honor the Yellow Emperor and the first dynasty of our history. Accordingly, we offer for your consideration the name 'Zhuangxiang.'"

"This is a well-constructed name. I will be King Zhuangxiang."

"Your Majesty, there is another matter which requires your attention."

"Continue."

"Your father, King Xiaowen, did not select a chancellor. That vacancy has been a burden to your government. We need someone appointed to this position."

"I have a man of talent that I have confidence in. His name is Lu Buwei. I desire that he fill this position and that all of you, in particular Lord Changan, serve me by helping him to learn the duties and responsibilities involved."

"Excuse me; Your Majesty … is this man not a merchant?"

"He is indeed a merchant, and I would be surprised if there is any nobility to be found in his family. I take that to be an asset. He is close to the people, and his perspective will be of value to the state."

Lord Changan looked around for a moment and finally replied,

"It will be as you wish, King Zhuangxiang."

* * *

When the court was dismissed, the Lord Secretary, the Minister of the Palace, and the Supervisor of Ceremonies remained. Lu Buwei was summoned. Lord Changan spoke first: "Your Majesty, tradition requires that you mourn your father. The mourning period is set at three years, although only twenty-five months is required. It has been arranged that you do not have to do any public demonstrations, and we will see that you only have to attend the internment if you wish."

The Supervisor of Ceremonies continued: "King Zhuangxiang, I will instruct your attendants on how to dress you. I would advise that you do not leave this building for any reason. People will be watching for any sign that you are not mourning. This could injure the performance of your office. The less you are seen, the better. Still, there is the matter of servants and others in the palace that might report an indiscretion. You should be solemn, refrain from music, feasting, and laughter, and have no contact with your concubines. If you have questions as to the proper action in any matter, I will be available to provide advice."

Lord Changan followed: "Again, by tradition, your government is to be administrated by the chancellor during the mourning period. Chancellor Buwei is, however, quite new, and I have no wish to take on this responsibility. I propose that you furnish a small room in your residence that is secure from both vision and hearing. There Chancellor Buwei and I may confer with Your Majesty and update you on matters requiring a decision. We will then issue the appropriate orders in our names. All reports will be sent to this same area, and we will follow any instructions that you may issue."

The new king found it was strange to hear his friend referred to as "Chancellor." But it was also satisfying. He and Lady Huayang had apparently won their "battle." He said, "I will cooperate anyway I can."

"I understand that the Queen Dowager will be advising you."

"'Instruction' is a better word. Yes, she has offered to assist me."

"It is a good choice. The Queen Dowager is both wise and experienced in these matters."

The Supervisor of Ceremonies had one additional instruction: "Your Majesty is required by custom to choose his coffin upon accession."

"My coffin?"

"Yes, Majesty. It is a tradition that is very old. There are usually three: an inner coffin and two outer coffins. You may, of course, change this, but the key requirement is to select what decorations and materials you desire. Tomorrow I will send craftsmen to you. They will provide you with assistance in making your selections."

The Minister of the Palace stepped forward and said, "With your permission, Majesty, I will lead you to your quarters."

"Yes."

He was led through the rear entrance, where they followed the enclosed walkway and entered the king's quarters. A large group of people were waiting. He was introduced to the attendants who all placed their foreheads to the ground. Next he was led to a small room, where his robes were removed and a team of Taoist doctors examined him. They pronounced the king to be in good health, with the minor exception of some swelling in the joints of his hands. An elixir was prescribed and he was dressed by the attendants.

CHAPTER 3

In early autumn of King Zhuangxiang's first year, his family arrived from Handan. Lady Zhao and Ying Zheng were treated as celebrities. They were provided rooms in the king's residence building, which was close to the palace courtroom. He found them both well. Ying Zheng was soon exploring the palace grounds with the curiosity and enthusiasm of all small boys.

Lady Xia was brought to Li Ziyan's house, where she was provided excellent quarters. Ziyan treated her as a treasure to be kept in honor and safety.

* * *

At first, Lord Changan was aloof and guarded with Lu Buwei. He was won over by the new chancellor's charm, respect, and humility. Buwei kept everything he already knew to himself and attended Lord Changan's instruction with expressed gratitude. For now they were pupil and teacher, but Buwei knew that Lord Changan would soon consider them as equals.

Together they toured the ministry departments. While most people would only see grand officials and their armies of well-dressed busy and apparently competent clerks, Lu Buwei saw the invisible people—the servants that served this aristocracy. These were, of course, dressed poorly, and many appeared unhealthy. Servants were almost always a challenge. They worked long hours in an environment of humiliation. As a result, they did exactly as they were told but absolutely nothing more. In the absence of direct orders, they were idle and often hard to find. Buwei could see the evidence everywhere: dusty corners and niches, neglected minor repairs, old paint, semi-clean latrines, small accumulations of trash, and general disorganization in hidden areas. They were all small things easily overlooked by the busy bureaucrats who saw the same environment every day. To Lu Buwei it was an excellent opportunity.

* * *

The Queen Dowager called on King Zhuangxiang at his residence. She was met by a guard and a servant. They escorted her to a room designated for the reception of dignitaries. The king entered and the Queen spoke. "It is time to improve your education, Your Majesty."

"Your instruction will be most welcome."

"I would suggest that you include the young prince, Ying Zheng. As Crown Prince, he will need to know what I can impart and more—even if he understands but a portion."

"I will send for him." A servant appeared and immediately sent off on the errand.

"Your Majesty, do you know why I was the favorite of King Xiaowen?"

"No."

"Well, I assure you it was not for my sexual skills. He had plenty of that talent available. No, I was the favorite because while he was Chancellor Lord Anguo, he relied on me for consul. I learned much, and I intend to pass some of that knowledge on to you and your son."

A few minutes later, Ying Zheng came running in. He halted in surprise at the presence of the visitor. His father said, "Ying Zheng, this is the Queen Dowager Lady Huayang. She is here to instruct us in important matters."

He had no idea what a Queen Dowager was, or the correct response, so he just bowed deeply to the Queen and looked back at his father to see if was all right to sit down. His father nodded and pointed to a mat.

"The principle job of a king is politics, and to be skilled you must understand the past."

Ying Zheng blurted out in excitement: "Master Confucius said to study the past if you would define the future!"

She leveled a blood-chilling gaze at him. He quickly realized his mistake and sat still with a deep blush. After a moment she said, "Yes, young Prince, he did say that. Now may I continue?"

No words were necessary, and she did continue: "The great Zhou Dynasty failed because they allocated lands to feudal lords who ended up declaring their own states when the dynasty became weak. The result was a confusion of over a hundred separate states. These then contended with each other. Many were conquered and absorbed by their neighboring states. Qin did not join this bloodbath until some 500 years ago, when the states of Shen, Zheng, and some Rong nomads allied to destroy the last remnant of the Zhou dynasty in the city of Haojing. Count Xiang of Qin led his troops to protect Zhou on its retreat to the city of Luoyang. They then returned.

"The eastern states continued to fight each other while Qin remained neutral. The present states of Zhao, Wei, and Han, on our eastern border, were then a single state named Jin. There was a famine in Jin 400 years ago, and its ruler, Duke Hui, asked for help. Duke Mu of Qin sent food and agricultural tools to Jin. The following year there was a famine in Qin, and they asked for help. Instead Jin attacked, trying to take advantage of our misfortune. Several battles resulted over the next few years. In the end Qin survived and managed to help Duke Wen become the new leader of Jin. Duke Wen was friendly to Qin but was succeeded by his son, Duke Xiang, who was not. While Qin was on a military expedition to Zheng, Duke Xiang ambushed and defeated the Qin army at the battle of Yao. Duke Mu retaliated three years later and defeated a Jin army, but did not take advantage of the victory.

"Now, some 200 years ago the state of Jin broke into present day states of Zhao, Wei, and Han. These three attacked Qin and killed Duke Li and took over a large part of our land west of the Yellow River. The duke was beheaded, and the skull was given to the Duke of Zhao, who used it as a drinking cup.

"Now, do you see a pattern here?"

Ying Zheng clearly wanted to respond, and the queen allowed it with a motion of her hand. "We were being good and everyone else was being evil," he said.

"Well, young man, in a sense that is true. It is a fact, however, that we were behind the times. Our battles were fought by nobles for noble purposes. The rest of the world was fighting war as a serious and bloody method for conquest. Armies were getting larger and larger. They were not commanded by nobles, and sovereigns stayed home. Instead the armies were led by professional generals and officers who did not seek victory but rather annihilation of the enemy. They accepted loss of their own men as easily as loss to the enemy. I can illustrate this with a story.

"Some 270 years ago there was a war between the states of Chu and Wu. As the armies faced each other, the Wu general lined up 3,000 condemned men in front of his army. He then gave an order, and all 3,000 committed suicide by cutting their own throats. The Chu army fled in fear.

"Another example is given in the *Six Secret Teachings*. Tai Kung tells us that a newly appointed general is to find the most powerful and honored man in the army and kill him in front of the troops.

"The sage Sun Tzu said it this way: 'To assemble the army and throw it into a desperate position is the business of the general.' In other words, the men of the army were expected to fight to the death. And today they do. Sun Tzu's classic tells how to do this and deliver decisive victories.

"Now, Qin was weak. It did not have a large population or large food resources. It did not have a professional army. If something drastic was not done, the huge armies of the east would devour it. This was one-hundred years ago.

"Duke Xiao changed all that. He retained a man named Wei

Yang. Under Yang's direction, the aristocracy was abolished in the feudal estates. The land was given to the people. Slaves were granted citizenship. People were resettled where their work would do the most to increase agricultural output. A system called 'meritocracy' was set up in the army. Promotion was no longer a matter of family connections; rather, a soldier advanced based on his own ability. The law was formalized and applied equally to everyone, and harsh penalties were exacted for minor offenses. Weights and measures were standardized, and other reforms were put in place.

"The effects were immediate. Yang led a military force against Wei, defeated an army led by the Crown Prince, and forced the return of the lands lost west of the Yellow River. The next time the bordering states combined to assault Qin, they were met at the Hangu Pass and defeated with a counterattack. The states of Shu and Ba were annexed in the south, increasing our land area, population, and food supplies. The forces of Wei and Han were decisively beaten at the battle of Yique. Zhao was defeated at the battle of Changping—that occurred while Your Majesty was a hostage in Handan."

The king spoke for the first time: "Yes—I remember that."

"We are no longer weak, but we still face large challenges. If you look at a map today, there are three primary areas of influence. There is Chu to the Southeast, Qin to the southwest, and the combined states of Wei, Zhao, Han, Qi, and Yan to the north. The forces of these areas are probably close to equal. Now, the northern states have allied together in the past and will certainly do so in the future.

"When there are three contenders, each will seek one of the others to help defeat the third. This is dangerous ground for the politician and the diplomat. Expect many offers both false and true. Expect subversion on every level. Remember what made us strong, and keep to that course." She paused, then said, "That is enough for today."

* * *

A few months later, the king called another private court after consultation with the three lords. A large table had been centrally placed in the throne room. When all were present, King Zhuangxiang took the platform in his mourning clothes and the Queen Dowager sat on his left.

The Lord Secretary then announced the meeting's single agenda: "Allow me to introduce all of you to the military and civilian governor of Shu—Shou Li Bing."

A small man entered with a large rolled document under one arm. He approached and bowed deeply before the king. The Lord Secretary continued: "Shou Li Bing has just completed the largest water project in history—the taming of the Minjiang River. I am told it is a marvel that can only be compared to the Great Emperor Yu's taming of the northern rivers in ancient times."

Li Bing approached the table and unrolled a huge map. Everyone, including the king, gathered around. Li Bing pointed out the main features: a large diversion dam; a river channel cut through Mount Yulei; extensive levees; an irrigation system providing the capability of growing rice in wet paddies; and a fairway to Chengdu for transporting food for the military.

"Does this wonder have a name?" the king asked.

"Yes, Your Majesty. It is called 'Dujiangyan.'"

"Zheng Guo is digging a canal across the Guanzhong Plain between the Jing and Luo rivers. With these two wonders, the people and the army of Qin will not hunger!"

* * *

As autumn continued, the Director of Agriculture's staff was busy day and night compiling the harvest. The numbers were good everywhere. Additional storage was going to be necessary. On hearing this news, the Grand Commandant immediately ordered the army to construct granaries.

Meanwhile the humble merchant, Li Ziyan, was visiting the nine Great Officers. They knew him well from his trade, but this was something new. He carried a letter of introduction from Chancellor Buwei that encouraged each minister and officer to give fair consideration to Li Ziyan's proposal. This was interesting. They all knew the chancellor could simply order the acceptance of any proposal. So they listened.

Li Ziyan offered to replace the servants of each chancellery department with people trained to complete all tasks in a professional manner. He would supply cleaners, cooks, carpenters, painters, grounds keepers, and any other personnel required. These persons would wear uniforms with a symbol sewn on the left breast. Ziyan would compile a list of tasks and frequency at the direction of each department. The workers would be organized into teams that could travel from department to department in the completion of similar tasks. Li Ziyan would assign foremen to supervise the work and receive any complaints or requests. All workers would observe protocol and keep all matters confidential, but would be expected to be treated with respect. Discipline would be handled by Li Ziyan himself, and punishment for the communication of even the most trivial would be death. The workers would live in the city and be housed in groups where each member would be responsible for reporting any indiscretion by another member. Finally, the cost of this service would come from the budget of the Chancellery.

It was a tempting offer, and every minister and officer accepted.

* * *

King Zhuangxiang summoned Lu Buwei to his quarters. It was late afternoon and the sky was darkening. They met in a reception room. The king welcomed the chancellor and said with a warm smile, "We have come far, Buwei."

"Yes, Ying Yiren—we have indeed come far."

"I need a favor."

"Anything, Your Majesty."

"I desire to see my mother, Lady Xia. Can you take me to Li Ziyan's house?"

Lu Buwei thought a moment before responding. "There are serious security concerns, but I think I can arrange a visit in safety. When would you like to leave?"

"This evening."

"Please give me two hours."

"That will be fine."

Precisely two hours later, Lu Buwei showed up at the royal residence with a peasant cart and driver. The cart had a large box structure with covered windows. The king slipped inside and they drove to the gate. The guards recognized Lu Buwei and immediately stepped aside. A few minutes later, they were at Li Ziyan's house. The king entered the house and found his mother waiting. She rushed to hug him with tears streaming down her face. Lu Buwei and Li Ziyan led the pair to the small conference that they used so often, then left the king and his mother alone. Lady Xia spoke first: "I have missed you very much."

"And I have also missed you, Mother. How are you?"

"I have been treated well. How is Ying Zheng?"

"He is well."

"I fear for both of you. You have been tools for people seeking power, and those people have elevated you to danger."

"What danger do you see?"

"That, I cannot say. I only know that the throne is too visible. No matter what you do, you will create new enemies in addition to those who already suspect the early demise of your father. I know that your soul is pure and that you were not given any choice in this series of events. But I would be happier if you and your son could have been left in a lower position and that I could have remained your mother."

The king was silent as his mother continued: "The Queen Dowager and I had a long talk. I understand and accept my position. I am an inconvenience. I am fortunate, so I have been told, that I am allowed to live. The life that I have, however, will be one of sadness and loss."

The king tried to speak but she stopped him with a wave of her hand. "I will be traveling with Shou Li Bing to Shu. There I am to be treated as a 'great lady.'"

"But Mother, is this necessary? Can't we find another way?"

"No. If anyone from the dynasty sees me, I will be recognized and the succession will be questioned—and if the succession is questioned the state will be in danger. This is the only way."

* * *

Li Ziyan's employees arrived at the chancellery departments and began work. As had been agreed, they were all well dressed in matched clean uniforms. They were polite, deferential, industrious, quiet, and good-natured. Worst of all, they smiled most of the time. This was disconcerting to many. The nobility had been removed from the countryside. It was only the army, ministries, and other court offices that still retained a significant number. Nobles expected their inferiors to be sycophants and their servants to be fawning and fearful. These workers had none of those characteristics. They showed pride in their work, no matter how menial it might be, and they required neither instruction nor orders.

But the results began to show. Before long the departments found themselves in environments that were not only clean and groomed but actually seemed new and somehow more professional. Other government departments were soon making requests for similar services from Li Ziyan.

Lu Buwei now had a network of eyes and ears to rival anything the Minister of Governmental Affairs and the Minister of National Espionage could manage together.

CHAPTER 4

Ying Zheng was required to attend classes every morning. These followed a prescribed curriculum of music, calligraphy, and reading assignments. He was, however, allowed free rein in the palace grounds almost every afternoon, and he took advantage of every opportunity to visit his favorite spots. Two palace guards followed him, often at a trot to keep up with the energetic eleven-year-old. One of prince's favorite spots was the Office of the Army. His curiosity caught the attention of Lord Biao, and he approved access to all areas except the Ministry of Strategic Planning, the Ministry of National Espionage, and his own office. Ying Zheng's favorite area was the tactical training classrooms, where new officers learned to handle companies, battalions, and regiments. It was fascinating. The rooms were filled with sand tables and small models of soldiers, chariots, and cavalry. These toys were far better than anything he had ever played with, and play with them he did. He was careful to not disturb classes in progress, but would sometimes listen to the instructors from the hallway.

One day, an instructor walked into the room where Ying Zheng was playing. "Your Highness, allow me to introduce myself. My name is Zhu Di. I am an instructor here."

"Yes, Sir. I am sorry—I will put everything back."

"No need to be sorry, young Prince. You may play anywhere a training room is available."

"Thank you, Sir."

"You are welcome. That is, however, not the reason I interrupted your play. I wondered if you would like some tactical instruction."

"Tactical instruction?"

"Yes. I can show you how to set the soldiers up and show how they are deployed for marching and fighting."

Ying Zheng beamed. "That would be great!"

"Good. Let's start with a company. From the tables over there, bring a chariot, four horses, a driver, and four officers. The driver is the one with his hands extended. The officers are the figures with armor but no weapons."

Ying Zheng rushed to the display stand, collected the figures specified, and set them on the table.

"Very good. Now we will need twenty crossbowmen and fifty infantry. I will help you."

Zhu Di helped Ying Zheng set up the figures on the table and counted them to ensure that the correct numbers were present. He then pointed to the chariot. "This chariot is special. It is not a war chariot; rather, it is the command center for the company. Let's set up the four horses that pull the chariot … fine, now place the driver and two officers in the chariot."

Ying Zheng complied and eagerly waited for the next instruction.

"Now, the company is divided into two platoons called the 'left' and 'right.' Divide the figures so that each platoon has one officer, ten crossbowmen, and twenty-five infantry. There are five men to a squad, but we won't worry about that now."

The figures were divided as instructed.

"Now let's arrange the company for a march. We have two platoons of thirty-six each. If we have them march four across, that will make nine ranks each. This will easily fit on most roads. So place your crossbowmen in front of each platoon, with infantry following and the platoon commander in the last rank. Place one platoon behind the other and lead with the chariot."

The instructor stepped back and watched the Crown Prince set the company up. Another instructor passed in the hallway and looked in. He was dismissed with a stern glance.

When Ying Zheng finished, Zhu Di inspected the company carefully. He adjusted a few figures and said, "Discipline is very important. You must ensure that your company marches in precise formation. There, that is better, don't you think?"

"Yes, Master."

"Now, let's set the company up to fight. Remember that the squad size is five. How would you arrange the troops?"

"I guess I would set the platoons side-by-side since their names are 'left' and 'right.'"

"Good, now how would you place the rest?"

"Well, I think some crossbowmen could shoot kneeling down while others could shoot standing up. So I would arrange the crossbowmen in two ranks of five each in front and the infantry in five ranks of five behind. The officer would be at the rear to give orders."

"Correct! Set up the company."

Zhu Di watched Ying Zheng set the company. He kept his face stern but he was smiling with satisfaction inside. The prince aligned each figure precisely so that the ranks and files were absolutely straight. He left a narrow space equivalent to one man between the two platoons. When he was finished he stepped back and smiled with pride.

"That is a good formation. Now, come over here at look at the company from the front."

Ying Zheng followed his instructor.

"Now, Prince Zheng, the sides of every formation are called the 'flanks.' As you face the company, your left is the company's right flank and your right is the company's left flank. Now which of these is the stronger and which is the weaker?"

Ying Zheng was puzzled.

"Look closely. On which side do the infantry carry their shield?"

"On the left arm, Master"

"Yes. And that is the weaker side. This means that when you attack you attack most strongly on your right flank. If you are forming your company on the flank of the enemy, choose your right flank in order to attack the enemy's left. At the same time, it means that the enemy can be expected to attack your left platoon first. You must train your troops to be able to rapidly turn and meet such an attack in good order. Now when the crossbowmen finish their volleys, they retire to the rear while the infantry engages. Where should they make their new formation?"

"Behind the left platoon."

"Correct. The crossbowmen from both platoons should form

behind the left platoon to defend a flank attack."

The prince stood proudly.

"You have done well, Prince Zheng. Please continue your play as long as you wish. You may want to set up another company and imagine how a battle might go. If you desire more instruction, I can be available."

"Thank you, Master Di. I would like to learn more." The prince continued his play until one of the guards reminded him that it was time for supper.

* * *

King Zhuangxiang summoned the Lord Secretary. When Lord Changan arrived, the king met him in the same reception room used for the Queen Dowager's instruction. The king spoke first: "Lord Changan, the private conference area will be finished in a few days. In the meantime, this will have to do. I require your advice."

"Yes, Your Majesty."

"I have been thinking about the remuneration for Chancellor Buwei. As you have already pointed out, he is a merchant. How can I raise him to the appropriate status?"

"There is the example of Wei Yang. When this philosopher came from Wei to Qin, he accomplished much, but did not have rank. Duke Xiao assigned him to lead an army against his former homeland, despite the fact that he had no military experience. The army encountered a strong force led by the Crown Prince Ang, of Wei. By fortunate coincidence, the two men knew each other. Yang set a letter to the Crown Prince.

"The content of this letter has been held as an example for the use of diplomacy and deception in war. It read: 'Originally I had friendly relations with you. And now we are the generals of two different countries. It is unbearable that we should fight each other, and so I suggest that we have personal interview, make an alliance with music and drinking, and desist from war, so that Qin and Wei may have peace.'

"The crown prince accepted the invitation and was captured by Wei Yang while the Qin army received its attack order. The Wei army fled with casualties. For this effort, Wei Yang was enfeoffed with the income of 10,000 households and granted the title 'Lord Shang.'

"Now, Chancellor Buwei has created a favorable impression for me. Your Majesty was correct—he does seem to be a man of talent. Like Lord Shang, he does not have military experience, but Qin has plenty of officers who can assist him. I would suggest that we meet with Lord Biao's staff, select an achievable military target, and charge him with taking it."

"This pleases me. Please set up a meeting with Lord Biao. I want to have the session at his headquarters. You and the chancellor will attend. Keep the subject matter confidential between you and myself."

* * *

The following day, the Queen Dowager arrived for another lesson. When the king and prince arrived, she began. "Today I want to talk about the nine rules for governing the state.

"The first is to cultivate your own character. It is of value to study virtue and seek knowledge, but it does not mean that others will see you as worthy. Be composed, dignified, and quiet, and people will think you to be a sage.

"The second is to honor men of virtue and talent. Find, honor, and retain the sage and the philosopher. Let all know that they reside with you. As for men of talent, hire them before another state does.

"The third is affection toward your relatives. Your clan is large. Your father left many concubines and sons and daughters. Your grandfather also left many who are still with us. They are the primary threat for internal conflict. This can start as simple gossip and intrigue but can grow to actual revolt and assassination. Treat them generously and watch them closely.

"The fourth is to respect the ministers. Watch your ministers closely. Form objective opinions of them. If they are worthy of respect, treat them with consideration, kindness and generosity. If not, kill them.

"The fifth is kind and considerate treatment of the whole body of officers. Know them and reward them frequently. Watch how they behave on the receipt of recompense and promotion. If they become arrogant, greedy, overbearing, or insubordinate, replace them. If they demonstrate benevolence, kindness, and virtue toward the people, replace them. The people need to respect and fear officials. Virtue is not an asset.

"The sixth is to deal with the mass of the people as children. Children have simple wants—food, clothing, shelter, security. Provide that by providing work. Children understand punishment, reward, and consistency. Punish small offense heavily so that there is no great offense. Apply the law consistently to all. Provide reward when warranted and in a way that is widely noticed.

"The seventh is to encourage the resort of all classes of artisans. The artisan and craftsman create many things of necessity and beauty. They provide things that others see when they observe the state. Challenge them to provide the finest, and reward them according to the value of their skill.

"The eighth is indulgent treatment of men from a distance. Create a state that other people want to join. When they arrive, welcome them and provide them with land or employment.

"The ninth is to treat the princes of the states kindly. This is the art of diplomacy. Be prepared to make allies with anyone who may provide an advantage. If alliance is not profitable, treat them with friendship until it is necessary to destroy them.

"To these nine, handed down from antiquity, I would add another: grow the three treasures in their proper order. First achieve great agriculture. When that is accomplished, achieve great industry—and if that is present, grow great commerce. Today, some would say that we have all three. That may be, but still follow the priority in augmentation."

Ying Zheng raised his hand for permission to speak. His father smiled because he knew the question before it was asked.

"Go ahead, young Prince."

"I heard of these rules in my instruction at Handan, but the meaning was described very differently. Master Confucius described a system founded on virtue and learning, starting with the ruler and ministers and extending to the people. Master Mencius wrote that all men share a sense of benevolence, righteousness, propriety, and knowledge of approving or disapproving.

They are, therefore, naturally inclined toward virtue, and value virtue in their family and superiors. Master Confucius had a saying regarding punishments; I fear I cannot quote it exactly."

Ying Zheng's father smiled again and provided the quotation: "'If the people be led by laws, and uniformity sought to be given them by punishments, they will try to avoid the punishment, but have no sense of shame; if they be led by virtue and uniformity sought to be given them by the rules of propriety, they will have the sense of shame and moreover will become good.'"

"Thank you, Father. Master Confucius also said, 'When the man of low station is well instructed, he is easily ruled.'"

The Queen Dowager looked at both men with a stern countenance. "I assume Your Majesty approves of the prince's desire for rhetoric?"

"Yes—I am quite interested."

Turning to Ying Zheng, she said, "Well then, let me respond first to your last quote. Lord Shang wrote, 'When the people are stupid, they are easy to govern!'

"The difference between these last two quotations sets the difference between our points of view. The main subjects seem to be: Is man inclined to virtue? Which is more effective: the rule by law and punishment, or the rule by virtue? Is it profitable to have a people that are well instructed?

"Now, young Prince, you might not suspect it, but I have read Mencius along with other sages. His argument is that, given man's natural desire for virtue, the existence of poverty and crime in a state must be due to the neglect of the ruler to provide conditions where virtue can be realized. In other words, the criminal is entrapped by the state, so how can the state punish him?

"To this, I answer that Master Mencius was naive. All men do not desire, or value, virtue. According to the *Classic of History* this was recognized in earliest antiquity from the time of the three sovereigns and five divine emperors. The Emperor Shun said that the mind of man is restless, prone to error, and its affinity to what is right is small. He spoke of the need to rectify the people's virtue through the use of the five punishments. Those five punishments are still used today. We have invented nothing.

"Then as now, the objective of punishment is to create a state where punishment is not needed because the people abide by the law. That is the reason for inflicting heavy punishments for small offense. Now all states, past and present, have laws. In each era, law is written as appropriate for that time. Since a people that follow the law in all respects can be said to be virtuous, the second question is moot.

"There remains the third—instruction to achieve knowledge. "Instruction will not be received equally by all. There will be those who cannot comprehend it from their own stupidity. There will be those who can comprehend it but choose to not follow. Even the best may falter. Again citing Confucius: 'Superior men, and yet not always virtuous, there have been, alas.' The only instruction required is knowledge of the law."

Ying Zheng broke in: "And you would deny the people knowledge?"

"What knowledge do they require? All know filial and fraternal duties. These are taught in the home. Ask any child to name the five duties and he will respond, without hesitation: 'Sovereign and minister; father and son; husband and wife; elder and younger brother; and intercourse between friends.' The only other thing needed is knowledge applicable to the trade to which they are born. A peasant farmer only needs to know the five kinds of grain and how to plow, sow, and harvest each. The woodcutter only needs to know the various types of trees and how to cut, trim, and transport each. Thus Lord Shang writes, 'Though there may be a bundle of the Odes and History in every hamlet and a copy in every family, yet it is useless for good government.'"

The king and prince were quiet.

* * *

The king arrived at Lord Biao's headquarters by a royal covered coach. He found the Grand Commandant, Lord Changan, and his friend, Lu Buwei, waiting for him. He approached the trio and announced, "Since this is my first visit, I desire a tour of the facilities before we begin the discussion of other matters."

"Certainly, Your Majesty. Please follow me."

Lord Biao led the tour starting through the training areas first. To his surprise, the king found his son in one of the rooms, with an instructor at his side. Ying Zheng was busy setting up miniatures on a large sand table.

"What is going on here?"

"Your Majesty, the prince has been coming here with some regularity. It started as play. Colonel Zhu Di has been teaching him some basic tactics—I am told that he is an attentive and gifted student. They started with company level maneuvers. Looking at the table, it would seem that he has graduated to battalion level.

The entire staff has become quite fond of him."

Ying Zheng heard conversation and looked up to see his father watching him with obvious pride. "Father … I am just …"

"Please continue your lesson, Son. I would be interested in learning from you."

The group moved on. They passed more training rooms and went into the office areas. There was one office that was quite interesting. A sign on the door announced that no one was allowed in. King Zhuangxiang tried the door and it was firmly locked. Turning to Lord Biao, he said, "Tell me about this office."

"That is the office of Sun Pin, the Minister of National Espionage. He is a very competent and skilled man. He knows information that is not shared with anyone, including myself—and I prefer that."

"I would like to see this man in his environment. Please arrange that. Tell him that I will share nothing."

An aide accepted the errand and they moved on. There was similar security at the office of Strategic Planning, but they were allowed entrance without difficulty. They entered a large room with an extensive map of the states and areas beyond, spread on a table. The king said, "I would like to conduct our meeting here."

Just then the aide returned and announced that Minister Pin was ready to receive the king, preferably alone. King Zhuangxiang immediately set off for the secret office.

Minister Pin met him at the doorway and bowed deeply. He was motioned inside and offered a mat. "Would Your Majesty like to have tea?"

"No, thank you," replied the king as he looked around the small office. There were two doors leading to other secret locations. The room itself was sparsely furnished with a desk and two mats. No papers were evident anywhere, but there was an interesting composition on the wall—a depiction of the *Nine Virtues* in large paired characters.

The king accepted the mat and waited for the minister to occupy the mat behind the desk. Minister Pin was very much an average man. He would be able to pass unnoticed almost anywhere. There was, however, brightness in the eyes that said this man was far from average.

As the minister was silent, the king opened the conversation. "You have a very interesting composition on your wall."

"Yes, Your Majesty. I think about the virtues every day. As you might imagine, the business we conduct here involves many things and many people. There are things we do and people we use that are … better left unknown. There is little room here for what others would call virtue, ethics, or honor. And yet the sage Sun Tzu writes, 'He who is not sage and wise, humane and just, cannot use secret agents.' Now the sage has virtue and the wise desire it. This is a profound paradox, and I ponder it frequently."

"I don't think I am wise enough to help," the king said. "It is very interesting, and I shall remember it. Now, Minister, what can you tell me of your department?"

The minister pointed to one door and said, "Beyond that door are a series of offices—one for each state and several other offices for special interests. This other door leads to what are called 'interview' rooms. Apart from that, there is little that I can share without a specific request."

"What information is available from these state offices?"

"We can provide detailed and summary information on a number of subjects: economy, population, military strength, politics, geography, food reserves, and other items of interest—without, of course, revealing our sources."

"Can you provide an indication of the capability to influence decision making?"

"Yes, Your Majesty."

"Do you have an office for Zhou?"

"Yes, Your Majesty."

"Thank you for your time, Minister. I will be calling a meeting in the map room of the office for Strategic Planning. I will see you there. Bring your officer assigned to Zhou."

Minister Pin rose and bowed deeply as the king left the room.

* * *

Ying Zheng was busy setting up the battalion. Zhu Di had provided wood squares so that each company could be moved as a group. There were two new kinds of troops: unarmored archers and spearmen carrying spears with a second blade extending out to the side. There were a number of full-sized versions of this weapon in the room.

"Master Di, I do not understand these spears. Why is there a second blade?"

"These are called dagger axes. They are used for thrusting, like an ordinary spear, but once the thrust is complete, they can be pulled back to inflict more damage. If enough force is used, that second blade can decapitate a man. They are mounted on staffs that can be as long as eighteen feet. Properly used by several ranks, these weapons cannot be defeated by cavalry or chariots."

"What is the next higher level above battalion?"

"That would be the regiment, each with twenty companies of infantry, five companies of dagger axe men, and five companies of archers."

"Wow. That would take a long time to set up!"

"Yes it would, and I would have to check to see if we have enough figures. There are more than 4,000 men in a regiment."

A messenger appeared at the door and passed a note to Zhu Di. A few words were exchanged, and then the messenger saluted and said, "Yes, Colonel."

Ying Zheng's mouth dropped. "Master, you are a colonel?"

"Yes."

"You command many men!"

"In battle, I command a division. That amounts to two or three regiments."

"Why do spend time with me?"

"Because, Prince Zheng, I like you. The next time you come, we will set up a regiment. Would you like that?"

"Yes, Colonel Zhu Di; I would like that very much!"

"I will find more figures, a larger table, and more people to help."

* * *

The group that gathered in the map room was larger than the king had expected. Besides the six men he had specified, there were another dozen from the Ministry of Strategic Planning and the chief of staff. More wanted to attend, but Lord Biao cut them off.

King Zhuangxiang opened the session: "Minister Sun Pin, please summarize the situation in Zhou."

The minister motioned to his Intelligence officer, who began: "Zhou has been in decline for a number of years. They still consider themselves to be the titular head of the states that, at one time, made up the dynasty, but they receive neither tribute nor recognition from those states. Their territory is very small, as can be seen on the map. There is a single city, Chengzhou. The population is, in general, leaving for other states. Their army is in disarray after the recent murder of its leader, Duke Wugong."

The king stopped the presentation. He was remembering the road trip with Lu Buwei. Buwei had mentioned that name as a "business matter." The king said, "Tell me more about this murder."

"Yes, Your Majesty. His body was discovered in an alley of Chengzhou. He had been stabbed several times. There were no witnesses, and no suspects have been arrested. The investigation determined that he was apparently on his way home after visiting a gambling hall. It was suspected that he had considerable debt."

"Please continue."

"Yes, Your Majesty. Our estimates indicate that the state could probably raise no more than 10,000 troops, and most of those will be untrained."

"Are there other states that might offer aid?"

"Wei, Han, and Chu all desire this territory, but they have been unwilling to attack it themselves. They might launch an attack masked as a relief effort. Actual assistance is unlikely."

"I desire to eliminate this state."

Lord Biao spoke. "When do you wish to have this happen?"

"The harvest is completed. Let's complete this before winter sets in."

"Yes, Your Majesty. I would recommend four regiments for the main assault, with two more in reserve. We can field this many without conscription and still secure our borders."

"Fine. The assault force is to be led by Chancellor Buwei."

Lu Buwei was speechless.

CHAPTER 5

The winter passed quietly. The private conference room in the king's quarters was completed. Lu Buwei's mission had succeeded—the state of Zhou no longer existed. The former merchant was enfeoffed with the income of 100,000 households. His new title was the Marquis of Wenjin. In court proceedings and in public, it was not proper to address high officials by their personal names. Within the new conference room, however, the king addressed his three lords as Secretary Changjio, Chancellor Buwei, and Commandant Biao.

The four men met almost daily. No matter how much time the three lords might spend watching each other's departments, here they treated each other with respect. Reports were reviewed, decisions made, and orders given as needed. The king was in mourning, so all orders were issued with the chancellor's signature. There had been no major scandals, apart from a few officials who had been caught serving other states as agents. This was expected to happen. It was, however, surprising that, in many cases, the compromised official was caught by the Chancellery before either of the other lords knew anything of the threat.

* * *

Winter was a busy time for the army. The nomads of the north and west liked to do their raiding during the cold months, when the frozen rivers provided highways for their mounted troops and the villages held stores of grain. This was both a problem and an opportunity. The need for a dispersed defense corresponded with the time that manpower could be taken from agriculture, with little effect on productivity. Thus the army did most of its training in the winter. Qin managed to create, in this circumstance, a body of peasants that were not only trained, but often had actual combat experience.

* * *

The mourning was not difficult. King Zhuangxiang had worn robes made of course woven hemp and hemp shoes for the first five days. They were certainly less comfortable than silk, but he did not mind. Protocol called for King Xiaowen to lie for five days before being placed in his coffin, and to be interred five months later. After the five days, King Zhuangxiang was dressed in the robes of autumn, which were of white silk. He wore a girdle and head cloth of woven hemp and a mourning cap. At the start of winter, the robes were exchanged for black.

The requirement for simple food was to his liking. This also varied by season. Autumn called for hemp seed and dog. Winter called for millet and pork. He had not formed any attachment for music, so that requirement was easy. As to the requirement to avoid concubines, that was also quite easy, since he had the required attendants and no others. His duty to his wife was not prohibited, since that duty was the third of the five obligations of filial responsibility. Most of the court women were confined in separate quarters and guarded by eunuchs. This was not the case with his wife or the Queen Dowager. These, along with his son, were quartered, at his command, within the king's residence.

Winter was normally hard on the king's hands. The swelling usually increased, the range of motion decreased, and there was almost constant pain. The new elixir, prepared by his doctors and taken twice daily, had worked wonders. He felt no pain, the range of motion improved, and the swelling was less noticeable. He began to suffer headaches, but the doctors provided a powder than relieved that discomfort.

* * *

Ying Zheng had spent much of the winter with Colonel Zhu Di. A large room had been found and additional figures made. With the help of ten other instructors, a full regiment, in battle array, had been set up. It was an impressive display and it would become a permanent part of the training academy.

His lessons focused on the details. One day as the prince was examining the figures; Colonel Di approached him and said, "Today I would like to talk about cheng and chi forces."

"Please"

"Most of what we have practiced with is cheng. These are the regular forces that are fixed by number and organization. We have now, in this display, added chi."

"Do you mean the cavalry and war chariots?"

"Yes, and others that you have not seen, such as praying mantis soldiers. The first important point is that these are the only types of forces. As there are only five musical notes, there are only two kinds of military forces. The variations on the musical notes cannot be counted. The same is true of the combination of cheng and chi."

"These figures formed to the side—are these chi?"

"They could be. The number of cheng is fixed; the number of chi is variable. The organization of cheng is fixed; the organization of chi is variable. Further, cheng can become chi and chi can become cheng."

"I have read these terms in the military classics. It is a confusing idea."

"As it should be. Now look at this smaller force beside the regiment. It is mostly chariots and cavalry. If an enemy were engaged with the regiment, this small force might decide the issue by attacking the enemy rear. That leads to the general rule, which is: engage with cheng and win with chi."

"How can chi become cheng?"

"The principle of chi is surprise. If the enemy knows that you will attack his rear and prepares accordingly, then the chi has become cheng."

"Is chi usually chariots and cavalry?"

"There should be nothing usual about chi. An infantry unit could be chi by attacking an enemy flank from a concealed position. Let me help you get some figures, and we will work through a few examples to start. But the best way to learn this subject is by examining actual battles."

Together with other students, the prince began to study recent battles. He soon learned that the range of history available for study was quite limited. Current armies were considerably different from their older counterparts. In Tai Kung's time, a division of 10,000 men fought with over 700 chariots of various types. The modern division of 10,000 men was primarily an infantry unit that had fewer than 150 chariots, and many of those were used as command vehicles. Colonel Zhu Di explained that chariots are limited by terrain and are ineffective against large, well-ordered infantry. The key is size.

* * *

Chancellor and Marquis Lu Buwei had been granted approval to start a project that he had long dreamed of: the completion of a compendium of all thought. Even as a merchant, Buwei had played with this idea—to take the often-acclaimed "hundred schools of thought" and replace the debate with some sort of consensus. He would begin to collect scholars as soon as the weather permitted. He already had his first—a very serious young man called Li Si. This man was an eloquent advocate of the school of legalism, which was the same school that framed the thought of Lord Shang.

When King Zhuangxiang approved the project, he remembered the Queen Dowager's words: "Find, honor, and retain the sage and the philosopher. Let all know that they reside with you."

* * *

The Queen Dowager continued her lessons. On recent sessions, the topic was court protocol, and for this instruction she included various persons, including the Supervisor of Ceremonies, the Grand Herald, and the Minister of the Palace. The number of rules was daunting: who should bow first, the correct response to a bow, what direction everyone should face, order of seating, proper forms of address and response, and a host of others—down to the correct response to a yawn. And all these rules varied with a number of different circumstances. It was all quite confusing, and the king had serious doubts if he could remember everything, particularly if he had one of his headaches.

Quoting Confucius, Lady Huayang offered some perspective: "'But while the important rules are 300, and the smaller rules 3,000, the result to which they all lead is one and the same. No one can enter an apartment but by the door.'"

In the end, a number of signals were arranged between the king and the Grand Herald to assist the process.

CHAPTER 6

The summer of King Zhuangxiang's first year had seen modest crops for Qin but widespread crop failures for its eastern border states. The state of Han and Wei suffered the worst, while in Zhao the shortage was mostly confined to the western area around Taiyuan. Minister Sun Pin noted this information and monitored the Yellow River closely throughout the winter and early spring. When it seemed clear that the river would have low summer flows, he announced to Lord Biao that this combination of circumstances provided a good opportunity for an offensive. Biao's staff had plans ready for just such a time, and the king was consulted. The attack began the summer of King Zhuangxiang's second year. The mission was assigned to General Meng Ao.

General Ao led a large force of four corps numbering 160,000. It required several days for the army to march through the Hangu Pass. The western defense of Han withdrew without a fight. The army moved east toward Luoyang and Chenggao and took the Hulao Pass after a brief skirmish. General Ao left a force of 40,000 troops to defend their gains and crossed the Yellow River with 120,000 troops. The Qin army then turned west and marched north to the Fen River valley. Again it found no opposition. The city of Anyi was taken. Another 40,000 troops were left in Wei, and the remaining 80,000 marched up the river valley and took Taiyuan, a major food producing area for Zhao. On the second anniversary of Zhuangxiang's ascension, General Meng Ao announced that he had taken thirteen cities in Han and twenty more in Wei. The report failed to note that most of these were villages and that a number of cities had been bypassed. Still, it all looked good on a map.

* * *

The twenty-fifth month after King Xiaowen's death passed, and the mourning was over. King Zhuangxiang abandoned the cap, head cloth, and girdle. He still wore the silks of the season, but the new robes were much more elaborate and embroidered with beautiful images. The color and decoration of the lower half followed the season. The theme for autumn was the color white with the white tiger as the divine creature. The decoration of the upper half was always a fu and axe head. He had a variety of new hats. The most important one had a horizontal rectangle with twelve rows of hanging beads in the front and back. This was reserved for court sessions.

The king found many requests waiting for him. Formal court sessions had been petitioned from foreign states and district governors. Chancellor Buwei was anxious to formally introduce the scholars he had collected. The king's extended family wanted a banquet. The Minister of the Royal Family was urging the king to select concubines—to both ensure successors and, interestingly enough, to extend his life. There were numerous sacrifices and ceremonies to be conducted. The Minister of the Palace was urging the Royal Hunts to resume. King Zhuangxiang learned that three were expected every fall. The first was to provide dried meats for sacrifices; the second was to provide meats for guests; and the third was to provide for his kitchen. There had been no opportunity to learn weapons during his exile. The king had to arrange archery lessons so that he could attend these hunts—and it turned out that he did have natural talent.

This was also the time for the king to advance his vision for the state of Qin. The only problem was that King Zhuangxiang did not have one.

* * *

In the midst of sorting all this out, Chancellor Buwei left the palace compound for a visit with his partner Li Ziyan. He needed advice.

Ziyan met him at the doorway and bowed deeply. "Forgive me. Do I address Your Lordship as Marquis of Wenjin or Chancellor Wenjin?"

"Call me your friend, Ziyan, and please take me to our little conference room."

The familiar routine was followed. They ordered tea and settled on the mats, then began to talk about anything other than the purpose of the mission. "I expected that you would be wearing finer robes … Friend."

"I had to slip out quietly. Otherwise I am accompanied by a

small army of guards and aides."

"I understand."

"So, Ziyan, has your business been good?"

"Yes, Friend, it has been satisfactory. I still get those fine bronzes from Zhao. I have also found a good market for high quality calligraphy—in particular wall hangings. I heard that the king's minister of spies has a set of the *Nine Virtues* hanging in his office!"

"Extraordinary! I have a young man living with me who would perform similar duties without reference to virtue. He is a 'legalist' and is quite firm in his opposition to Confucius."

"There are probably many differences in these two philosophies. But they do agree on one thing: they both despise merchants. Your experience is remarkable! You are the only merchant I know of to have climbed from the bottom to landed nobility. For the rest of us, we must be happy with our money!"

Both men laughed, then Lu Buwei continued: "I must admit that the nobility part of all this was expected, to a certain extent, but I was most concerned when they put me at the head of an army. Now that it has happened, I want to do something truly noble, something that I will be remembered by. I have already started a project that should provide Qin with a status enjoyed by no other state."

The tea was served. After a few moments, Lu Buwei said, "Li Ziyan, I require advice on a lady."

Li Ziyan looked puzzled but remained quiet, so Lu Buwei continued: "Several years ago, I purchased a concubine named Zhao in Handan. She was young and lovely, with many appetites. Apart from a desire for extravagant clothes, jewelry, and other fine things, she had a large sexual appetite. As you know, I brought Ying Yiren into my house as a future investment. This young man was quite taken by the lady, so I gave her to him. He subsequently married her, and they had a child named Ying Zheng."

Li Ziyan interrupted: "Friend Buwei, is there any chance that this offspring was yours?"

"I have heard rumors to that effect, but unless a woman can carry a child in her womb for over one year it is impossible."

"Thank you, please continue."

"You are aware of subsequent events. Ying Yiren became King Zhuangxiang, Ying Zheng became Crown Prince, and Lady Zhao became the queen. Lady Zhao did not want to have any more children and took familiar contraceptives to ensure that would be the case. Her sexual appetite was still very strong, and she professed to want more than her husband supplied. She approached me for a continuation of our prior arrangement, but I deferred."

"A wise decision."

"Yes. She may have had other liaisons prior to becoming queen, but if she did, she was discrete. After becoming queen, she was located in the king's quarters and, as you can imagine, indiscretion is very difficult there. She repeated prior offers, and I again deferred."

"Your career, and your life, would have been destroyed."

"I thought everything was going fine and she could satisfy herself with her husband. This changed, however, when the king's mourning period ended. The king was advised to select a large number of concubines. He was told that with each sexual encounter he could obtain some of the woman's 'Yin' and this would increase his 'Yang' existence. This, in turn, would prolong his life. It was recommended that he spend no more than two nights each month with his wife and to spend the remaining nights with as many concubines as possible. It was an offer that few men would reject. The queen expressed no outward objection, but she was furious, and that fury turned on me. She insisted that I had put her in this situation and that I must find a solution."

Li Ziyan thought for several moments, then replied, "This is dangerous. Is she close to her son?"

"No. At Handan she surrendered the boy to servants as soon as she could, and the boy has separate quarters here with his own company of servants."

"Then the best course would be to arrange her death."

"There are three reasons for excluding this option. First, she is quite the flower, and I would hate to lose her. Second, it is too near the time of King Zhuangxiang's father's death. Her sudden death would raise a storm of speculation. Finally, I do not know how much of this is known to her ladies-in-waiting. They could be expected to maintain confidence while she is alive, but—"

"So, Lu Buwei, are you suggesting that we find her a male harem?"

"No. That would not work. Palace security is too good. What is needed here is a single man of exceptional ability, one who could arrive and depart without much notice. Perhaps a daytime stud would work."

"Such a man could be found. Men with 'ability' tend to have extreme pride and tend to boast. It would be wise to look for a candidate in remote regions where a reputation is known only to locals. I will see what I can find." Li Ziyan mused with a smile on his face.

"Friend, what do you find so amusing?"

"You are a strange man, Lu Buwei. Here in a single conversation we have spoken of noble projects and, at the same time, have plotted to deliver a stud to a whore!"

* * *

The three armies prepared to winter. The forces in Han chose nearby Xingyang as their quarters. The forces in Wei selected Anyi, and the main force wintered in Taiyuan. Food stocks had run low and supplies were slow from Qin. The peasants in the countryside had very little following a year of famine, and the Qin army took what little they had. It was a very hard time for the population, and deaths from starvation were considerable.

* * *

The required hunts were completed, much to the delight of the people allowed to hunt for themselves as they followed the king.

The Grand Herald drafted court schedules and submitted the requests to the Minister of the Palace. There were five courts scheduled for each ten-day period. All sessions were held in the morning and normally followed the same order: first, the reception of foreign envoys; second, the presentation of new sages and philosophers; third, audiences with district governors; fourth, the reading of reports to be approved for inclusion in the Royal Library; and finally, a time for presentation of all other approved issues.

As the Queen Dowager has predicted, the foreign envoys all

carried proposals for alliance and peace with the new King of Qin. Over time, King Zhuangxiang had seen envoys from King Huanhui, of Han; King Anxi, of Wei; King Kaolie, of Chu; King Xiaocheng, of Zhao; King Jian, of Qi; and King Xi, of Yan.

Gifts were exchanged, and all requests were received politely with no promises given. Repeat appearances were made by Han, Wei, and Zhao, with requests for the return of territory occupied by the Qin army. These last began politely and gradually escalated to demands.

* * *

Li Ziyan found a candidate for Lu Buwei. The man's name was Lao Ai, and he did have quite the reputation. Now it was necessary to determine how to get this man access to Queen Zhao. The chancellor had no choice but to involve the Minister of the Royal Family and the Supervisor of Attendants. Both men were sworn to secrecy.

Queen Zhao was absolutely thrilled with her new stud.

* * *

When summer arrived, it brought danger. A combined army of all forces available from Wei, Zhao, Qi, and Yan counterattacked General Meng Ao's main force. It was led by a general from Wei called Wuji. Farther south, Han conducted a desperate counterattack on Xingyang but failed. General Wuji's army numbered over 100,000 and the Qin army defended with difficulty. General Ao was wounded leading an attack, and the army began a withdrawal back down the Fen River valley, abandoning the city of Taiyuan. General Ao's forces found suitable defensive positions and engaged the allies. General

Wuji split his army to defend Taiyuan and pursue the Qin army. Both could not be done, and General Ao's troops held their ground.

General Wuji proclaimed the relief of Taiyuan a great victory. General Meng Ao was taken to Xianyang to recover, and the command was turned over to General Wang Ji.

* * *

The following fall, General Meng Ao died, as did the Queen Dowager Lady Huayang. The king was once again in mourning, and the pressures of court were relieved.

The subsequent winter was hard. The king began to suffer from diarrhea, and more medicine was prescribed. He also suffered from frequent drowsiness and was unaware that he was slowly being poisoned. The elixir that was so helpful to his hands contained arsenic, and that metal was slowly accumulating in his body. The end came in the third month of spring.

The State of Qin now found itself with a thirteen-year-old king. It would require seven years before the young man could be "capped" and assume authority.

CHAPTER 7

It was widely believed that King Zhuangxiang had been poisoned—and that was, of course, absolutely true. The popular suspect, however, was the young king's regent—Chancellor Buwei. This man must have ambitions on the throne itself.

As for Lu Buwei, he was as free from such a desire as he was innocent of regicide. The king's death was, for him, very inconvenient. Virtually all of his ambitions had been satisfied. He was rich and titled. His only unfulfilled desire was to leave something that would be remembered after he died. That "something" was his project with the scholars of the "hundred schools of thought." He had collected 3,000 respected philosophers for this project and had the complete support of King Zhuangxiang. That cherished endeavor was now in danger.

The problem was that Qin had never had a king this young. Over the last hundred years there had been five kings of Qin, and the youngest had been nineteen on ascension. He had little choice on the matter of regency. Tradition carried the weight of law, and that tradition was clear. Whenever the king was unable to govern, whether for illness, mourning, or youth, the government was to be administered by the chancellor. Few had ever expected that such temporary control could last for seven years. There were very likely to be challenges for the throne, and a successful challenge could well bring death to himself and his project.

* * *

The rush of events was all very confusing to Ying Zheng. He had known that he would become king one day, but that would be much later. Now, in a matter of an hour, he was told that his father had died and that he was king. Servants were already changing his clothes for fine embroidered silks. His hat and shoes were changed, and a new girdle was tied.

He looked up and saw Lu Buwei enter the room. "Uncle, what do I do?"

"Relax, Majesty. You do not have to do anything. You are excused from mourning because of your age. Likewise, you are not required to run the government because that is my duty as your regent. The most important thing, right now, is that you look like a king—and I see that has already happened!"

* * *

Lady Zhao was now Queen Dowager. She'd hardly ever seen her son before and would see even less of him now that he was king. That meant more time with Lao Ai, which was fine by her. Before long it became clear to her servants that she was pregnant. A reason would have to be found for her to leave Xianyang until the child was delivered.

A clever ruse was devised. The Queen Dowager reported that she was having repetitious dreams that showed a man with fire emanating from his body. An oracle had advised that this was the Yan Emperor and that he was requesting a pilgrimage to his tomb.

Legend reported that man was first ruled by three divine sovereigns: Fuxi, Nuwa, and Shennong. Of these, Shennong, the flaming one, was also known as the Yan Emperor and was a contemporary of the Yellow Emperor. His tomb was near Yong, a short distance west of Xianyang. There the Queen Dowager would stay until the divine one was satisfied. This would surely bring good fortune to the state of Qin.

The story was not just accepted, it was cause for celebration. As Lady Zhao left on her mission, the population showered her with gifts and cheered her as a hero. Her entire staff, and Lao Ai, accompanied her.

The mission lasted six months, and a son was left in the care of servants at a secret location.

* * *

The first year of King Zheng's rule was largely about learning what other people expected of him. The Supervisor of Ceremonies was almost always at his side, ready to whisper advice when needed. Lu Buwei made a point of visiting him at least once daily. Otherwise he did not see the regent except at court. He was not asked to make any decisions—or for that matter, to speak to anyone at all. At court he was to sit on his mat and observe. The chancellor sat on his right and the Supervisor of Ceremonies sat on his left. He attended temple sacrifices with a large armed escort and followed the whispered directions.

There were, of course, mistakes. Once he yawned at court, which resulted in everyone politely leaving. At one banquet, he was enchanted with the entertainment and forgot to eat. As a result, nobody ate. He occasionally bowed inappropriately. This would result in the recipient quickly stepping aside to decline the honor.

In general, the king was expected to remain in his residence and the attached court and banquet rooms. He was provided access to a private courtyard for archery practice. Apart from that, an escort was required, and the king had to use one of the royal coaches. He requested approval to continue his military studies with Colonel Zhu Di. Lu Buwei advised against it for the time being. To the king's surprise, a tactical training room was hastily added to the residence building so his request could be met. Before long, the colonel was able to resume the king's instruction.

Two years later, the king received sexual instruction from a beautiful and talented concubine. He resumed the fall hunts and was allowed to accompany Lord Biao on an inspection trip of the winter training.

* * *

The three lords meeting had changed considerably. King Zhuangxiang had been able to foster an atmosphere of cooperation between the heads of his government. King Zheng had not yet attained these skills. Each lord began to keep more and more information to himself and this, in turn, led to mutual suspicion. Lord Changan felt like the odd man out on many occasions.

Of the many issues under discussion, the war in the border states occupied at least a part every meeting. General Wang Ji had been unable to advance and was finding it increasingly difficult to maintain his position. The problem was supplies. The route for foodstuffs and equipment followed the Fen River from Anyi to the army's location south of Taiyuan. The area was crawling with bandits and much was lost or damaged before reaching its destination. Severe retributions were dealt in every village and town along the route but had no effect. Patrols had been dispatched to catch the bandits, but with mountains on both sides of the valley, the rebels had many places to hide.

General Wang Ji reported that he would withdraw to the border of Wei and Zhao in order to shorten his supply route. Lord Biao was furious but had no choice but to trust the commander's decision. He began to talk of reinforcement, and the chancellor went along with that option even though it would cause a shortage of labor in agriculture. Still, Lu Buwei urged that the relieving force be no larger than was absolutely necessary. They settled on three corps. The commandant and chancellor named the secretary to lead the mission. It was an honor that could not be refused.

Lord Changan was now convinced that he was being plotted against. The mission would be hard and dangerous. It would be easy to arrange his demise. He began to suspect everyone.

* * *

In the summer of King Zheng's fifth year, Lu Buwei delivered his masterpiece. It was a monumental work consisting twenty-six scrolls divided into 160 sections. It was a cohesive syncretic statement of the thought of Legalism, Confucianism, Mohism, and Taoism. Its title was an expression of pride—*Lushi Chunqiu* (Mr. Lu's Annals).

The twenty-six scrolls included twelve "almanacs," eight "examinations," and six "discourses." The content covered philosophy, government, music, and agriculture. It contained over 100,000 characters. A copy of completed text was displayed in the market at Xianyang. One thousand measures of gold were offered to any scholar who could add or subtract even a single character.

* * *

That fall, the Queen Dowager made a second pilgrimage to Yong. A second son would soon join his brother in hiding.

* * *

King Zheng waited in the private conference room that his father had used for meetings. He had spoken to Lu Buwei about learning strategy. While his tactical training had progressed well, he was still concerned about turning battlefield success into actual conquest. He had little confidence in the Ministry of Strategic Planning and, considering Qin's recent history, that opinion was certainly justified. Uncle Buwei had reported that he had a very good teacher who had helped in the composition of the *Lushi Chunqiu*. He was bringing this sage to the king for a private audience.

Lu Buwei entered the room accompanied by a man who was certainly well past eighty years old. "Majesty; allow me to introduce a most wise man—Wei Liao-tzu."

The scholar bowed deeply and accepted a mat. The king offered his question: "Our General, Bai Qi, captured the capital of Chu but did not win the state. He defeated Han and Wei at the battle of

Yique but did not win those states. He defeated Zhao at the battle of Changping but did not win the state. Why?"

"Your Majesty; I can best answer with a story of Confucius: One day, the Master and his students passed a grave where they saw a women weeping at a gravestone. She told Confucius that her husband, her husband's father, and her son were killed by a tiger. When Confucius asked her why she didn't leave such a fated spot, she answered that in this place there was no oppressive government.

"Now the tiger, in each of three cases that you relate, is the state defeated. The oppressive government is Qin. In particular, it is Qin as led by Bai Qi, who was reported to have killed 890,000 persons and was called 'Ren Tu'—human butcher."

King Zheng said, "Is it not necessary to crush the enemy's army to take the state?"

"Yes, Majesty. General Qi, however, killed even after victory. He also killed persons not in battle, stole the people's food, and destroyed their property."

King Zheng replied, "Did not Sun Tzu write, 'Thus the wise general will concentrate on securing provisions from the enemy. One bushel of the enemy's foodstuffs is worth twenty of ours …'? And did he not counsel to distribute spoils of plunder to the army?"

"Yes, Majesty. Now you desire to conquer other states. What do you desire from this conquest? Is it not the people and the resources?"

"Yes."

"Then why destroy something you desire before you can possess it? Sun Tzu was most wise, but he was wrong in this instance. To conquer a state you must preserve the fields and orchards, refrain from plundering towns or disturbing the populace, leave the people means of livelihood, and secure their welfare. Your objective is to minimize enemy opposition and encourage surrender to a humane ruler.

"Send your civil authority with your army. Remove the fief lords, grant the people land, establish your laws, and ready your punishments and rewards. Then none can withstand you."

"Your words are indeed wise, Master Liao. I desire that you remain with us as my advisor on these matters."

* * *

In the seventh year of King Zheng's rule, Lord Changan received his commission and assumed command of 60,000 troops divided into three corps of 20,000 each. The army followed its orders and marched north toward Hancheng, where floating bridges had been placed across the Yellow River, at the point where the Fen River added its water to the greater river. Before reaching this objective, however, Lord Changan ordered a turn northwest and brought the army to Yanan. Just north of this city was Qiao Mountain, site of the tomb of the Yellow Emperor, Huangdi. Here, the lord made his gamble. Assembling the army, he delivered a speech that had been rehearsed many times with his commanders and staff.

"I am Ying Changjio, grandson of the great King Zhaoxiang, son of King Xiaowen, and brother of King Zhuangxiang. I speak to you as Qin is locked in a war with Zhao, Wei, and Han. This war has gone on for over seven years. It robs our strength and kills our people. And yet it was not sanctioned by any king of Qin. This war was started while King Zhuangxiang was in mourning. The authors are Lord Biao and Marquis Wenjin, acting in the absence of royal authority.

"These two have placed the army in a position that has caused the death of many men, including General Meng Ao. The men of Qin and General Wang Ji have defended extended positions heroically while suffering from bandits, weather, and hunger. Lord Biao and Marquis Wenjin have ordered you to join these positions and share their fate. We are then ordered to attack Taiyuan and take the city. The walls of this city are strong, and it is defended by Wei, Zhao, Qi, and Yan. We have already lost this city once, and our longer supply lines will help the enemy.

"I speak to you now, in the hearing of the spirit of the Yellow Emperor, and tell you that I will petition King Zheng to halt this unauthorized war. I take full responsibility for this action."

The speech was met with silence, and that satisfied Lord Changan.

* * *

Lu Buwei summoned Li Si to his office. The chancellor been very impressed with this young legalist. He had been very helpful in the completion of the *Lu Chunqiu*. Li Si had demonstrated skills in calligraphy, composition, and editing. Lu Buwei had assigned him to a scribal position in the Ministry of State. Now he needed him for a different composition.

Li Si entered and bowed deeply without speaking. After both men were seated, Buwei began: "Li Si, I require a composition. King Zheng will be 'capped' soon. Several members of the Royal Clan and others will petition the king to remove all foreigners. I have a draft copy: 'People from the feudal states who come to serve Qin in general merely travel here to cause dissension in Qin on behalf of their own rulers. We request the complete expulsion of all aliens.'

"That category would, of course, include both of us. I expect the petition to be one of the king's first agenda items. Ponder this threat and give me a response that I can present to the king."

"Yes, Chancellor—I will begin immediately."

* * *

King Zheng was "capped," and as a recognized twenty-year-old adult, assumed full powers. He was immediately confronted with many issues, of which two were primary.

First was the issue of Lord Changan's revolt. This was an administrative disaster. He had one lord questioning state orders and accusing the remaining two lords of crimes. The facts of the case were quite plain. His father had authorized the war on the bordering states, and using the excuse of mourning to question the authorization was simply wrong. The current stalemate could rightly be blamed on Lord Biao, but that was not the issue. A command had been ignored. This required firm immediate action, and King Zheng was up to the challenge. He dictated written orders to recall General Wang Ji. The general was to assemble forces, attack and defeat the forces at Yanan, kill Lord Changan and all his officers, kill any soldiers and city residents who offered resistance of any kind, and report back to the capital. There were to be no captives or trials. Victims were to be buried where they fell. Lord Changan was stripped of all titles and his lands confiscated. His family was banished to Shu without assets. Separate orders were issued for the execution of his three ministers. He dictated the orders in level tones, without emotional inflection. Lu Buwei recommended one of his scholars as replacement secretary—Feng Ji. King Zheng approved the appointment and moved to the next order of business.

The second issue was a petition to remove foreigners from Qin. The king had no intention of doing this, but he allowed his chancellor to present argument. The letter composed by Li Si was read to the court by the Grand Recorder.

> *Your servant has heard that when the lands are broad, grain is plentiful; when the state is large, the people are multitudinous; and when weapons are strong, men of action are valiant. So Mount Tai does not reject the soil, and therefore it can complete its size; the rivers and seas do not choose the tiny streams that flow into them, and therefore they can increase their depth; kings do not repel the masses, and therefore they are able to make their virtue continue to shine forth. Thus the earth will not have four quarters, the people will not have different countries, the four seasons will be replete and beautiful, and the ghosts and spirits will send down blessings. This is the reason why the Five Emperors and the Three Kings were without enemies. Now in fact you are getting rid of the black-headed people so as to provide a resource for enemy countries, and you expel aliens so as to build up the strength of the feudal states. You are causing public servants from all under*

heaven to hold back and not venture to turn their faces towards the west, to halt their feet and not enter Qin. This is what is called "contributing weapons to brigands and presenting provisions to robbers."

Now articles which are valuable although not produced by Qin are many; and public servants who wish to show their loyalty although not brought up by Qin are numerous. If you now expel aliens so as to provide a resource for enemy states and reduce your people so as to increase your foes, then you will not only be making yourself empty at home but also sowing the seeds of resentment in the feudal states. If you aim for the state to be free of dangers, this cannot be achieved.

King Zheng was quite impressed with Li Si's composition and ordered it to be included in the Royal Library. The chancellor was ordered to promote the young man to department manager. The Commandant of Justice was selected. One of Li Si's first tasks was to investigate strange rumors coming from Yong.

CHAPTER 8

Lu Buwei was understandably very concerned about the investigation. He considered many options, but there was no way out. The Lady Zhao had been a thorn in his side for years. Now she was going to destroy him. He had once loved her and, in a way, he still did. There were few others who could compare to her beauty, and even fewer who could match her narcissistic hedonism. Now that had been combined with an egotistical idiot – Lao Ai.

It was time for a final meeting with his friend, Li Ziyan.

Lu Buwei wore his full robes and dismissed his escort. He walked through the streets of Xianyang in broad daylight, creating quite a disturbance as he proceeded to Li Ziyan's house. The formalities were followed as before, and the two men sipped tea. Li Ziyan could tell something was very wrong.

"Friend Ziyan, we are undone," Lu Buwei said.

"What has happened?"

"Your stud, Lao Ai, has proven to be even more stupid than we imagined. The fool has decided to play the role of a displaced noble with means. He calls himself the 'Marquis of Shanyang' and claims to be a refuge from Yan. He has become known in Yong for his parties, where he has bragged that he has fathered two sons who will succeed the king. The report has reached the government, and the Commandant of Justice has begun an investigation."

"Can anything be done?"

"I'm afraid not. I appointed the commandant myself. He is talented, sincere, and incorruptible. All will be discovered. I would advise that you assemble your family and leave Xianyang as soon as you can."

"Will you also leave?"

"No—I am too visible. I have no choice but to stay and accept my fate. My family is in Wei and they should be safe. My only hope is that the *Lushi Chunqiu* survives."

* * *

Lu Buwei was reading reports in his office when the Minister of State, Wang Wan, and the Commandant of Justice, Li Si, entered and placed their mats before the desk. "Chancellor, we are here on a matter of great importance." announced Wang Wan.

"Yes, I know."

"Our concern at this point is how far this scandal reaches. Beside the Queen Dowager and this Lao Ai, we know of your involvement, along with the Minister of the Royal Family, the Supervisor of Attendants, and a merchant called Li Ziyan. Who else is a party to these events?"

"No one else is involved that I am aware of. There would, of course, be servants, the queen's ladies-in-waiting, and the retainers of Lao Si."

"We understand that this man has a thousand retainers."

"I do not know—I accept your numbers."

"How do you think we should proceed in this matter?"

"There is only one course. You must present the evidence—all the evidence—to the king. I will arrange a private audience with his majesty before this day ends. I will remain here and await his judgment."

"Yes, Chancellor."

* * *

King Zheng was furious over the embarrassment that attached to the incident. A strong force marched on Yong. Lao Ai was taken and killed, along with his retainers. The two children were placed in sacks and beaten until dead. The Queen Dowager was kept under house arrest. Lao Ai's family was found in Nanzheng and killed to the third generation. The Minister of the Royal Family and the Supervisor of Attendants were executed.

Lu Buwei was stripped of titles and banished to Shu. He left in a cart that was virtually identical to the cart that he had used to travel from Handan to Xianyang. He was replaced by the Minister of State, Wang Wan.

* * *

One day in Shu, a servant reported to his lady that there was a man in the street asking for her. The lady looked out of a window and recognized the man. Immediately the entire household was put in action: food and tea were prepared, the already clean rooms were swept again, the best mats were unrolled, and the lady changed robes. The man was escorted to the best room of the house. There, Lu Buwei was reunited with Lady Xia.

"Thank you for seeing me, Lady Xia."

"You are most welcome, Lu Buwei. Please regard this house as your home. You brought me into your house at Handan when I was in exile. It would honor me to return that gracious gift."

"I accept your offer with deep humility and gratitude."

* * *

Lu Buwei spent almost an entire year with Lady Xia. It was a happy time. There were long pleasant conversations in the garden. Visitors were entertained. These included a number of scholars offering praise for the *Lushi Chunqiu*. Shou Li Bing was a frequent visitor, and he gave them both a tour of the Dujiangyan project. Lu Buwei was satisfied that his life had been full. He had no regrets. And it was a bright and warm summer afternoon in Shu when Lu Buwei took poison and died.

PART II
Conquest

CHAPTER 9

King Zheng continued the purge of his government. Lord Biao was exiled. Execution orders were issued for all three army ministers. The only person to escape was Chief of Staff General Fan Yuqi, who fled to Yan.

The tactical training room attached to the royal residence was converted to a command center. There the king intended to exercise direct control over the armies. He would be both king and Grand Commandant.

Li Si had called for increased efforts to politically destabilize the other states. As a result, he was named the Minister of National Espionage and named as a court captain. The sage Wei Liao-tzu was assigned as the Minister of Strategic Planning. General Meng Yi, grandson of General Meng Ao, was given the task of chief of staff.

While he was making these changes, King Zheng decided on one more issue. He wanted a new palace. It was to be the largest in all the states. Its name would be Xin.

***

The king was urged to take time to decide on how he was to be buried. He refused to consider any details except one. King Zheng informed the Supervisor of Ceremonies that he wanted full-sized models of soldiers—enough to demonstrate for eternity the majesty of an entire Qin Division. The supervisor was instructed to get the details from Colonel Zhu Di. He would decide other matters later.

***

Construction was started on a new army headquarters. The building would be attached to the command center and would include offices for ministers and their staffs. The old facility was to be expanded and used as a training academy. It would be the largest facility of its kind ever built.

While the construction was underway, the ministers were housed in the king's residence building. When Li Si was looking over the offices of Sun Pin, he noticed, with some amusement, the wall hanging with the *Nine Virtues*. For reasons he did not completely understand, he took the hanging with him to the new office.

At the first meeting in the new command center, the king and his ministers stood over the central table, which now held a large map of the states. Miniatures had been placed showing the current positions of General Ji's four corps.

The king spoke first: "General Biao and his staff started this war with Han, Wei, and Zhao. It was approved by my father. General Meng Ao led the initial assault and achieved some success, but the effort stalled. General Wang Ji has been holding the ground gained ever since. This territory has not profited Qin. It produces very little and costs much to supply with food and equipment. The cost to deliver support is high due to bandits and other resistance. General Yi, I ask you to explain this."

"Your Majesty, it is my opinion that the forces allocated were not enough to accomplish the mission given. The resistance can only be due to people's hope that their states will eventually retake the territory lost. The mountainous terrain makes it difficult to extract these criminals."

"And why would they prefer their previous rulers over us?"

"Because, Majesty, we are the one with an army on their territory."

The king turned to Wei Liao-tzu and said : "Minister Wei Liao-tzu, please inform us as to the reason for this difficulty."

Wei Liao-tzu addressed the group: "I will repeat the words I have provided the king in answer to this question: To conquer territory you must preserve the fields and orchards, refrain from plundering towns or disturbing the populace, leave the people means of livelihood, and secure their welfare. Your objective is to minimize enemy opposition and encourage surrender to a humane ruler.

"This does not mean the army must fight with a dull sword. The army is to be an awesome force that will surely destroy any defense without pity. Make surrender the enemy's only option.

"Civil authority should travel with the army. Remove the fief lords, grant the people land, establish your laws, and ready your punishments and rewards. Then none can withstand you and there will be no resistance."

The king spoke: "This is the way the army of Qin must fight.

Make it a new regulation and enforce it with maximum punishment for violation.

"Now, I ask a different question. During what season did General Ming Ao conduct his assault?"

General Meng Yi replied, "General Ming Ao conducted his campaign in the summer and fall. General Wuji of Wei conducted his counterattack the following summer."

The king then asked, "When do the states conduct their military training?"

"The traditional time for training in most states is the autumn, Your Majesty."

"And when does Qin train?"

"Qin trains in the winter, Your Majesty."

The king replied, "Is this not an advantage? I have witnessed our winter training. I observed a regiment perform battlefield maneuvers in a blizzard. I doubt that any other army could perform such a feat as well. This advantage has not been used. General Meng Ao spent the winter in comfortable cities. Now tell me how we are to break this stalemate."

Wei Liao-tzu said, "The army requires major reinforcement. That reinforcement should be made centrally and amount to two forces with at least 200,000 men each. It is my understanding that the two best generals available are Li Xin and Wang Jian. These men should relieve General Wang Ji. Station one army for an attack on Taiyuan and a second army that can attack either central Wei or Han. Make the buildup deliberate and patient so that Li Si's resources can report the reaction by the states."

The king replied, "Then proceed." The ministers were dismissed and the king returned to his quarters.

* * *

King Xi of Yan did not know what to do with General Fan Yuqi. He had already withdrawn his army from the alliance and was hoping for peace. A renegade general could be trouble. He did believe there was some advantage in the fact that his son had been friends with King Zheng while they were both hostages in Handan. He chose to ignore the general's presence and sent his son, the Crown Prince Dan, to Qin as a hostage. There the prince might be able to reach an accommodation.

King Zheng was not impressed and he remarked to Chancellor Wang Wan, "This man is a professional hostage. I don't think he knows how to do anything else. Give him simple quarters and adequate food to survive, nothing more. Tell the guards I will be happy if he escapes."

* * *

In the tenth year of King Zheng's rule, and the third since assuming full power, Qin began building its forces in Wei. In the north, General Li Xin was assembling a force to strike up the Fen River to Taiyuan. Farther south, General Wang Jian was assembling an army near Anyi. This force was intended for an assault on Wei or Han. Together the two armies would comprise 500,000 men. Every officer and soldier would receive training in the new regulation.

The buildup caused concern in the entire area. In Han, King An had been on the throne for just three years. He was still consolidating his authority. He summoned his cousin, Han Feizi, a noted legalist with fifty-five published books. His works were known and respected in Qin. The king proposed that Han Feizi travel to Qin and offer the surrender of those lands already occupied by Qin, and to offer the remaining as a vassal state. While Wei did not offer to become a vassal, it did offer to surrender the lands occupied thus far.

Zhao reinforced General Wuji with additional troops from both Zhao and Wei. General Li Xin's army was watched closely. General Wuji was confident that, given equal force, he could defeat any Qin army on the plains of Taiyuan.

Wei Liao-tzu counseled that the weakest state should be struck first. Judging by the offers received at court, that state was clearly Han. Accordingly, Han Feizi was imprisoned and General Wang Jian readied his army for a crossing of the Yellow River.

Before the march was begun, an earthquake struck Han. There was widespread discussion on whether this was good or evil omen and, if so, to which side did it apply. Wei Liao-tzu was quick to respond to General Wang Jian: "What does an earthquake know of the conduct of men? There are no such things as omens, lucky or unlucky days, fortunate or unfortunate signs, or any other superstition. Conduct your action as ordered, and the outcome will be determined by your men, not the heavens or earth."

The army completed crossing the Yellow River and entered the Hulao Pass. The forces already in Han moved to the border with Chu to ensure there was no interference from that quarter. Luoyang had been heavily damaged by the earthquake, its walls having fallen in several places, and the city surrendered without a fight. The capital at Yangzhai was surrounded, but the siege only lasted a month before King An surrendered. Resistance in the rest of the country was minimal. In Xianyang, Han Feizi committed suicide by poison. The state of Han was no more.

A second earthquake followed the defeat. Chancellor Wang Wan's bureaucrats went to work immediately. With the assistance of the army, they distributed relief supplies and repaired damage while they dismantled the fiefdoms and reorganized the countryside.

King An was delivered to Xianyang, where he became the first ruler to be an honored prisoner of King Zheng. A team of engineers were sent to study King An's palace. An exact replica was to be built on a hill north of the Qin capital. The histories of Han and other documents were moved to the Royal Library.

* * *

General Li Xin and General Wuji matched each other man-for-man and horse-for-horse throughout the summer. Each side tried to hide reserves, but the spies soon found them out. By the start of autumn, it was clear that further reinforcement was futile. Any battle between Qin and Zhao would be fought with equal numbers.

General Li Xin waited until the second month of winter to start his advance. There was no opposition at the border, and the march north was uneventful. General Wuji had selected his battleground—a broad plain southeast of Taiyuan near the little village of Pingyang. There his entire force waited.

The two armies closed in a light snow storm. The Zhao forces were deployed in two ranks of a hundred divisions each. The divisions were formed in squares. Dagger axe men were spread across the front, with archers and crossbow men set before them. The cavalry and war chariots were split between the two flanks and located to the rear.

The Qin army's infantry formation matched its opponent. The dagger axe men were massed behind each flank, and the archers were located between the infantry ranks. Crossbow men were spread across the front. The cavalry and war chariots were consolidated some distance from left flank and marched ahead of the infantry.

General Xin's force advanced to the steady beat of huge drums. Visibility began to decline as the snowfall increased.

General Wuji moved his left flank cavalry and war chariots to the opposite flank and placed the combined force between the enemy and the infantry right flank.

As the two armies closed, the Zhao army delivered heavy volleys of arrows at the front ranks. The Qin army was not able to match the rate of fire because their crossbowmen had to fire while advancing. Men fell, and the Qin army marched over the bodies. The drums continued their beat.

Front rank archers and crossbow men retired and the Qin infantry engaged the enemy dagger axe men. Here the infantry had some advantage. The dagger axe was effective against cavalry but less so with the infantry, which could brush aside the weapons with their shields. Still, both sides suffered casualties.

On the Zhao right flank, the cavalry and war chariots from both sides sparred, looking for advantage.

The drumbeat increased in volume and frequency as the snowfall increased and combined with a wind from the west. The rapid drumbeat was a signal to General Xin's chi: the second rank of infantry. These ran to the right and around the left flank of General Wuji. Meanwhile the Qin archers focused their fire on the same flank. General Wuji ordered the second rank forward in support. The Qin infantry continued to advance along the flank while the first rank advanced with fury. The front line of the battle began to approach the shape of an "L," with the short side extending deep into the Zhao left flank. The short side of the "L" began curling inward like the rolling-up of a bamboo mat. As it rolled, the Qin archers adjusted their fire by following signal arrows fired ahead of the flanking infantry.

Confusion increased in the Zhao army. The infantry heard shouts and clashing weapons behind them, before them, and on their shield side. Each man could see his companions but little else.

General Wuji lost communication by flag in the storm. Reports from runners indicated a failure on the left flank. He needed to assess the condition of his army. The Zhao gongs were struck to order a withdrawal. Order was impossible in the blinding snow. The withdrawal turned into a rout with men running anywhere away from the drums which continued to beat. The Qin army held their positions.

When the storm cleared, General Wuji collected the troops he could find and withdrew to the east. Taiyuan was left behind. The Qin army surveyed the field: 100,000 Zhao and Wei dead lay in the snow. General Xin's losses amounted to 10,000.

Taiyuan was taken with little collateral damage. The towns and fields were mostly undamaged. As in Han, the civil authorities set about reorganizing the country, providing aid, and setting up a Qin administration. The army repaired damage where found and assisted in food distributions.

The entire campaign and consolidation was completed by King Zheng's fifteenth year of reign. The territory added was considerable and was already contributing food and manpower to the army. The ground gained was defensible, and there were no reports of bandits or insurrection.

CHAPTER 10

Crown Prince Dan escaped. His only injury was pride, but that injury ran deep. He was humiliated by the total disinterest of King Zheng, the condition of his quarters, the quality of his food—and most of all, the fact that the king did not even give him a respectable guard. He could easily walk away, and so he did. Prince Dan wanted revenge.

When he reached Ji, Prince Dan learned that Qin's General Fan Yuqi was in the city. The prince found this man and brought the general to his residence. Fan Yuqi found the prince to be a gracious and generous host. The only thing he seemed to want in return was information on the court of King Zheng.

Prince Dan also sought the counsel of his former tutor, Ju Wu. He wanted to meet a man with many friends of mixed reputation. He was advised to seek a retired official named Tian Guang.

Tian Guang loved to entertain and be entertained. He was known for his eclectic collection of guests. Among his current guests was an odd trio that he had discovered in the marketplace.

The trio consisted of a self-proclaimed swordsman/scholar from the old state of Wey named Jeng Ke. His companions were a dog butcher from Yan and a skilled lute player named Gao Jianli. The trio was quite fond of wine, and when drunk Gao Jianli would play his lute while Jeng Ke sang in harmony and the dog butcher danced.

All would soon meet.

* * *

Li Si had provided gifts to a number of officials—and more than a few ministers—of the various states. These were carefully measured so that they were not so large as to arouse suspicion, but large enough to guarantee compromise should the source be revealed. With these assets, the Minister of National Espionage could ensure that any message he desired was delivered.

For now, that message was quite simple: "There has been animosity between the state of Qin and Zhao for over a hundred years. It began when Duke Li of Qin was killed and his skull was used as a drinking cup by the Duke of Zhao. The insult resulted in almost continuous warfare between the two states. At one time or another, every state has joined with Zhao to attack Qin. The state has, however, survived. Qin's famous general Bai Qi defeated Zhao but, with help from Wei and Chu, Zhao defeated the Qin generals Wang Ling and Wang Ho at Handan. Today, Qin's hatred of Zhao has increased a hundredfold because King Zheng was born a hostage to Zhao and spent his first ten years as a prisoner in Handan. The continual support of Zhao has cost all the states dearly. The time has come to accept that King Zheng will revenge himself. The state of Zhao will fall to him. It cannot be prevented. There is little to gain, and much to lose, in continuing to support Zhao. Let King Zheng have his revenge, and this will satisfy him. Remember that the state of Han lost its existence over its support of Zhao. Do not share this fate."

The message resonated in Wei. General Wuji had left the coalition forces and returned with what was left of his army. Wei had paid dearly and was now weakened. It was easy, in such circumstances, to forget that their goals had matched Zhao's for years. They both coveted the rich land west of the Yellow River. Now with this new perspective, Wei could dismiss this all as a misguided attempt to support a criminal state. Ambassadors were instructed to offer support to the just cause of King Zheng.

Yan agreed with its minister's corrupted council because it was perhaps the weakest of all the states. Qi agreed with the implanted message for a different reason. Although relatively small, Qi was one of the strongest states. Its eastern position allowed it to wait and observe the course of events. It intended to conserve its strength and use it only when needed for its own benefit.

Chu was a different matter. In terms of numbers, it was a very strong state. Its government was a different story. The government of Chu was filled with a host of competing voices. Its ministers and officers were corrupt and self-serving. Chu's king was weak and incapable of providing leadership. Li Si's message joined a number of other opinions including that of several generals who wanted to invade Shu and Ba while Qin's attention was focused in the north. For the moment, the only impact of the message was to add to the confusion. The most likely outcome was inaction, and that was satisfactory.

Zhao received a different message. There, Li Si's agents were urging the remaining military to seek a decisive battle with General Xin. The new commander was General Li Mu, and it was difficult to imagine this man seeking major battles. General Mu had gained his reputation defending Zhao from the Xiongnu nomads of the north. His tactics had used the indirect and "soft." He seldom presented a direct target and often took advantage of ambush. He frequently defeated isolated Xiongnu units, and the nomads were never able to hold territory for long.

When this news was reported to Li Si, he brought it to the attention of the war council. Wei Liao-tzu stated that to oppose the indirect and "soft" it was necessary to use the direct and "hard" in much higher numbers. Accordingly Chief of Staff General Yi ordered General Wang Jian north to join General Xin.

* * *

At Ji, in Yan, King Xi was in private conference with his prime minister, Yue Kuang. The meeting had been requested by Minister Kuang.

"Majesty, I have been informed by Grand Tutor Ju Wu that your son is planning insult to Qin."

"What sort of insult is Prince Dan planning?"

"Ju Wu did not know. He told me that he strongly advised against any kind of offense unless the state could first obtain reliable allies. He even suggested that the prince send emissaries to the Khan of the Xiongnu. The prince replied that he did not have enough time for diplomacy. Ju Wu then advised the prince to remove General Fan Yuqi from his household. Having this person in his house was like being the 'meat thrown in the path of a hungry tiger.' The prince also refused to consider this and asked to see someone with many acquaintances. Ju Wu suggested a man named Tian Guang."

"I have heard of this man. I understand he recently committed suicide by cutting his own throat."

"That is true. Please allow me to present the known details."

"Proceed"

"At my request, the Minister of Justice assigned men to observe and follow Tian Guang. They reported that Guang went to the Crown Prince's residence and had a private meeting with the prince. Afterward, he returned to his house, where he had a meeting with three of his guests. This meeting was also private. Tian Guang then retired to his room, where he told his servant that he was in possession of a state secret which could never be disclosed. To show his determination to honor this confidence he would, in the servant's presence, commit suicide. If the effort was not successful, the servant was to finish him."

"This is most interesting."

"Yes, Your Majesty, most interesting. There is more. Following Tian Guang's suicide, the three guests moved to the Crown Prince's residence."

"Who are these people?"

"A swordsman named Jeng Ke and two companions."

"What is your conclusion?"

"Your Majesty, I believe the Crown Prince is plotting to assassinate King Zheng of Qin."

"If that happened, it would certainly cause disorder in Xianyang. It would probably result in the recall of the Qin armies now in Zhao."

"And if it fails, we will all be meat for the tiger."

"Perhaps not. We do not really know anything. Let my son continue his mission. If it succeeds, we will enjoy the benefits. If he fails, we can disavow any knowledge of it and present his head as proof of our innocence."

* * *

The campaign in Zhao had become frustrating for both General Xin and General Jian. The Zhao forces under General Li Mu moved constantly avoiding contact. Whenever a Qin vanguard was used, it was usually ambushed and defeated. Occasionally the Qin armies would find their baggage trains raided or destroyed. General Mu successfully avoided traps and efforts at encirclement. The Zhao forces conducted a number of night raids, where a force of unknown size would attack the army camp and kill a number of Qin soldiers before disappearing. As time went on, it was becoming clear that the Qin army was not making any progress toward the conquest of Zhao.

Li Si constructed an elaborate and ambitious plan. All resources were employed. Expendable agents were sent with false messages; evidence was manufactured; reports were intercepted and changed; and rumors spread. By the time the corrupted ministers joined in, King Youmiu of Zhao could only reach one conclusion—General Li Mu was going to revolt.

The general was recalled to Handan, arrested and executed. The army was taken over by General Huan, a man of little experience but good connections at court. Under his leadership the army of Zhao massed and confronted General Wang Jian north of Handan. General Li Xin brought his army on the rear of the Zhao force. The battle was over in a few hours.

King Youmiu surrendered. His stepbrother, Prince Jia, fled to the small northern territory of Dai where he claimed a throne as King Dai. Qin ignored him and proceeded to incorporate Zhao as its own. The pattern begun in Han continued: King Youmiu was sent to Xianyang as another honored prisoner; and engineers prepared to build a replica of the Zhao Royal Palace at the Qin capital. Histories and documents were moved to the Royal Library.

* * *

Jeng Ke entered General Fan Yuqi's quarters and requested time alone. The general accepted and when everyone else had left, the two men sat on facing mats. Jeng Ke opened the conversation:

"The way Qin has treated you, General, may be described as atrocious. Your father and mother and your kinsmen were all put to death because of you. Now I hear that a price of 1,000 catties of gold and a city of 10,000 households has been put on your head. What will you do about it?"

Fan Yuqi reflected. He had not heard any reports of death in his family or among his friends. His only crime had been a failure to inspire the confidence of his king. It was a normal hazard of being in that high position. Ministers were not simply removed from power; they were executed so that they could not have any influence on the state. Multi-generation killing was reserved for the highest crimes and usually only applied where there was a threat to the state. Still, his escape from execution did raise his crime. What Jeng Ke was telling him could be true.

As to the reward, he accepted the fact of 1,000 catties of gold, but the enfeoffment was highly unlikely. That procedure was reserved for newly made royalty. Clearly this Jeng Ke was exaggerating in order to make some point.

Regardless, he was in a desperate and unhappy situation. The question, *What will you do about it?* haunted him every night. Finally he answered: "Every time I remember this, I always suffer pain to the very marrow of my bones, but when I make plans, I do not know what to come up with, and that is all there is to it."

Jeng Ke replied: "If I have a single utterance which may relieve the state of Yan from distress and take vengeance on your enemies. what about it?"

"What is this utterance?"

"I would like to get hold of your head so as to present it to the King of Qin."

Fan Yuqi was stunned at first, and then filled with ambivalence. He had to admire Jeng Ke. The man had solved the problem of obtaining an audience with King Zheng. The presentation of an escaped minister's head would bring the king close enough to allow an attempt on his life. Still they were discussing his head. He had fled to Yan to keep that item. It was apparent that he was expected to commit suicide so that the decapitation could take place. Was he in enough distress to do this? If he did not grant Jeng Ke's request, would he be murdered? Either way it seemed he would lose his head. There was the hope of an appeal to the

Crown Prince. Somehow he did not feel that would accomplish much. If he did go along with this, he would surely be remembered. Would that remembrance be that of noble motive or a fool? The thoughts raced on and on.

In the end, there was one overwhelming fact that could not be ignored. He was a soldier. All soldiers were trained that, in battle, if you seek your life by flight, you will lose it, and if you seek death by confronting the enemy, you will live. He had fled.

General Fan Yuqi stood without a word and cut his own throat.

* * *

In the first month of winter, Jeng Ke reached Xianyang with one companion. The man's name was Qin Wuyang. This man was reported to have killed his first man at the age of thirteen. He was to be the backup for Jeng Ke's attempt. They carried a map of Yan and the casket with Fan Yuqi's head. Inside the rolled-up map was a dagger coated with poison.

They were conducted to the palace. No one was allowed to carry weapons in the court, except for the king, who carried a long sword. The armed guards assembled at the base of the steps searched their furs carefully. Jeng Ke and Qin Wuyang climbed the seven steps and waited outside the double doors of the court. They were announced by a palace cadet named Meng Jia:

"The King of Yan is truly alarmed at the Great King's awesomeness and does not dare to raise troops in order to resist the officers of your army. He wishes the whole state to become a vassal and join the ranks of the other states in presenting tribute and acting like provinces and districts, so as to be able to have the honor to protect the ancestral temples of the previous kings. In his terror he does not dare to present himself, but he has respectfully cut off Fan Yuqi's head and put it in a casket and sealed it up. With it he presents a map of Dukang in Yan. With his salutations, the King of Yan dispatched these things from the audience chamber and has sent an emissary to report to the Great King. It is for the Great King to give him instructions about this."

They were summoned. On entering the courtroom, Qin Wuyang took one look at the room, the court officials, and the Great King in his robes seated before the giant screen, and he broke down. He trembled violently and could not move. The map case was in his hands.

Jeng Ke offered an apology for his companion, but it was cut off by King Zheng: "Get hold of the map case he is carrying."

Jeng Ke set down the casket, retrieved the map case, and brought it forward. King Zheng unrolled the map and the dagger was exposed. Jeng Ke grabbed the dagger with his right hand and grabbed the left sleeve of the king with his other hand. The king jumped back as the dagger was raised and tried to pull his sword with his right hand. The long sword failed to clear its scabbard. Just then, the king's left sleeve tore off and King Zheng fled around a pillar. Jeng Ke pursued him as the courtroom turned to chaos. The king struck Jeng Ke in the chest with both fists clenched together. At the same time, the assassin was stuck by a medical bag thrown by the doctor. This gave the king time to draw his sword, and he cut Jeng Ke in the thigh. Jeng Ke threw his knife but missed. The king inflicted seven more wounds on the assassin before the guards arrived and finished him off. As he died, they heard him utter the name of Crown Prince Dan. Qin Wuyang was still frozen in the same spot and was killed there.

The king, still breathing heavily, ordered the armies in Zhao to attack Yan immediately.

* * *

King Xi heard the news of the failed assassination attempt on the same day he learned of the Qin invasion. The king prepared to move to the Liaodong Peninsula in the northeast. The lute player, Gao Jianli, and his companion, the dog butcher, moved to Songzi in Chu. There they disappeared into the ranks of household servants.

General Wang Jian advanced his army toward the Yan capital of Ji. General Li Xin advanced on Xiadu, the "second" Yan capital. The combined cavalry of both armies advanced to the north. The Yan army, commanded by General Wan, moved to the frozen Yishui River at a point between the two cities. His army numbered 150,000. There he met two corps of General Jian, each numbering about 50,000. Two more corps marched well behind the vanguard.

The armies faced each across the frozen river, and then General Jian ordered the advance. As the armies clashed, the Qin army began to slowly withdraw back across the river. The Yan army maintained contact. When the entire Yan army had committed to crossing the river, the Qin cavalry appeared in a mad charge downriver and into the Yan flank. The horses came at a full gallop down the ice. The speed of the attack caused panic in the Yan ranks, and the formations disintegrated as men fled. At this point the withdrawing Qin corps turned and engaged. The last two corps advanced in support while a vanguard from General Xin found positions to the rear of the Yan force. The defeat was complete.

By the start of the third month of winter, King Xi and Prince Dan had fled. Both Ji and Xiadu were cut off from any support or supply. There was little available for defense of the cities, and both capitulated soon after the next year began. Apart from the narrow strip of Liaodong Peninsula, the state of Yan did not exist.

General Wang Jian turned over his army to his son, General Wang Fen, and left for Xianyang, hoping for a well-deserved retirement.

CHAPTER 11

General Li Xin remained in Yan to supervise its conversion to a Qin province and to continue the attack on the Liaodong Peninsula. General Wang Fen moved his force to Handan, where reinforcements were waiting. The state of Qin now had nearly two million men under arms.

Wei Liao-tzu had indicated that the next state to be taken would be Wei. It was the weakest state at this time, and its central location between the former states of Zhao and Han would provide geographical stability. On the diplomatic side, a formal complaint was made to Wei for hiding the conspirators of the assassin, Jeng Ke. The Wei ambassadors assured King Zheng that they would search for these criminals.

Li Si's agents focused on the state and reported anything that might be of interest. The current king of Wei was named Jia. He had assumed the throne following the death of his father, Jingmin. This occurred the same year as the fall of Handan. His capital was at Daliang, on the south bank of the Yellow River. The new king clearly intended to conduct a defense centered on this city. The bulk of the army had been brought there, the city walls were being augmented, new moats were being dug, and granaries were under construction. This, combined with the natural defenses of the Yellow River, meant that any siege would be a long event.

General Wang Fen had no intention of besieging Daliang. He also had no intention of following the proven tactic of winter campaigns. He had something completely different in mind.

* * *

Once work was completed on the Xin Palace, the king ordered his government to occupy it. The only exception was the army staff. Their new building was completed, and it was not far away.

The main gate of the new palace faced east and was wide enough to allow three royal carriages to pass at once. The gate was flanked by large square observation towers of four stories. Inside was a paved terrace that measured seventy-five steps on each side.

The court building was on the north side and was approached by two sets of nine steps with a broad platform in between. It was here that the palace guard kept watch. The color scheme was the same as the previous court but in reverse. The exterior was brilliant white with green columns supporting the overhanging roof. The wood carvings depicting the heritage of Qin in the old palace were repeated here in bronze.

Inside the courtroom the walls were black. The ceiling was eighteen feet high and was also painted black. It was decorated with small silver stars. The inside pillars were the deep red of cinnabar. The building had two roofs, and between them were windows on all four sides that flooded the courtroom with light. The floor was polished stone. Column tops and bases, on both the interior and exterior, were yellow. The king's platform was elevated five steps.

The screen behind the platform was larger and spoke of King Zheng's ambition. It included the same symbols as the previous screen. To these were added the imperial symbols of the Zhou:

The sun as the symbol of enlightenment
The moon as the symbol of heaven
The Constellation of Three Stars as the symbol of the universe
The mountain as the symbol of stability
The five-clawed dragon as the symbol of power
The pheasant as the symbol of literary refinement
A pair of bronze Goblets as the symbol of loyalty
Seaweed as the symbol of purity
Grain as the symbol of prosperity and fertility
Fire as the symbol of intellectual brilliance

Together with the fu symbol and axe head, these made twelve.

The residence building for the king and his family was connected to the rear of the palace and included a number of banquet halls. Connected to this structure were separate buildings on the right and left of the palace. The one to the right was the conference room for discussions with the three lords. The one on the left was the Army Command Center.

Facing the palace across the terrace was the Royal Library. It was the largest building in the entire palace complex. This was the office of the Grand Recorder. Under him were three officers: The Recorder of Interior, The Recorder of Exterior, and the Recorder of Attendance on the King. Each of these had his own library. In the front hall of the library was a large room where the scholars of broad learning could read library volumes and compose discourses and commentaries. The Library of the Interior contained the histories of Qin, the records of census, the records of production, provincial reports, and other documents related to the state. The Library of Exterior contained copies of the books of Confucius, Mencius, Mozi, Han Feizi, Lao Tzu, Zhuangzi, Sun Tzu, Tai Kung, and many others. It had, of course, several copies of the *Lushi Chunqiu*. The histories and documents of Han, Zhao, and Yan were found there. It also included the secret records of the Ministry of National Espionage. The last library contained records all court sessions and mandates issued.

At the west end of the terrace were situated temples to the five divine kings.

Streets running north/south were connected to the terrace. These led to an area behind the library where the offices of the Royal Secretary were located. The area behind the palace contained the offices of the Chancellery.

A wall surrounded all of this and extended west along the hill facing the Wei River. Here the palace of Yangzhai, Handan, Ji, and Xiadu were placed. Covered walkways connected all these, with a rear entrance to the king's residence. Space was allotted for more.

* * *

King Zheng was in no hurry to attack Wei. The important thing was to prevent interference from Qi and Chu. For this he needed

Li Si to keep up his program of propaganda and subversion. Again Li Si's argument was simple: "Wei has continually allied itself with the criminal state of Zhao to attack Qin in their lust for land west of the Yellow River. They have not only supplied assistance, they have actually sent generals to lead these criminal attacks. Now they have added the insult of hiding the conspirators of an assassin who tried to kill the king of Qin. These injustices can no longer be tolerated. King Zheng is justified in his demand to remove the threats to his territory, and to punish those criminals who dared to endanger his life."

The patience worked. After two years, it was clear that Qin would have a free hand. The occupation of Wei was seen as inevitable.

A strong protest was made for the failure to deliver the criminals, and the Qin army left Handan. It was early summer. The army numbered 400,000 men. In addition to their weapons, every man carried a pick, shovel, or other tool. The cities of Ye and Wei fell in rapid succession. The army moved on to the Yellow River. An encampment was made on the northern bank east of Daliang. On the opposite bank, 100,000 Qin soldiers from the former state of Han appeared.

The troops immediately went to work on a dam. A diversion spillway was dug first, to allow the free flow of the river. The dam was then built. The riverbed was filled with rock to divert the water to the spillway. By the time of the annual freeze, a wide base had been constructed to the height of the water. This base was then raised to the desired height. The labor took almost a year, and the dam's height was easily comparable to some city walls.

When the spillway was filled the next spring, the Yellow River began to rise. As it rose, the riverbed was exposed below the dam. General Wang Fen crossed with most of his army and took positions south of Daliang. The city flooded. The city walls of packed earth might have held the water, but all fortifications require gates, and these were smashed by the rising water. Refugees fled south. All unarmed citizens were granted free passage. Persons of wealth, officials, and those in army clothing were detained. Eventually King Jia appeared and surrendered. The dam was dismantled and the Yellow River resumed its normal flow. The damage to Daliang was not repaired, and the city was abandoned.

King Zheng now had three kings in Xianyang, and a fifth palace replica would find its place along the hill to the north. Again the histories and documents were moved to the Royal Library.

* * *

King Zheng held fewer court sessions than previous kings, perhaps one or two every ten days. Those that did take place were mostly receptions for new provincial governors who technically reported directly to the king but, in practice, were managed by the chancellor and secretary.

Virtually all other business was conducted in private. Daily meetings occurred in the king's conference room with Chancellor Wang Wan and Secretary Feng Ji. The subject of these meetings was the pacification and incorporation of the conquered states. The civil authorities that followed the army had followed their orders thoroughly. Fiefs had been dismantled and their assets transferred to Xianyang. The land had been redistributed among the peasant farmers. All taxes were forgiven for at least two years. In some areas with distress, the relief extended for three years or more. These measures, while very popular, cost little. The assets taken from the government and nobles more than covered the lost revenue.

Qin's laws had been posted everywhere, and those who could not read were instructed in hamlet meetings. All this created a huge need for civil workers. King Zheng wanted to mollify the face of Qin authority. Accordingly, men of talent and worth from Han were assigned civil positions in Zhao while such men in Zhao were assigned civil positions in Yan and Wei.

The first task of these new officials was to collect census data. Each home was visited, and a list was posted outside that provided the names of all persons in that household. The family was responsible to keep the list current with births, deaths, and any other changes. These same changes had to be reported to the local authority. Local courts were instituted to hear disputes and to judge offenses. Registrars were employed to record population, land allocations. and production. Constabularies and administration were established. The Ministry of Governmental Affairs, under the secretary, was expanded to keep an eye on these new public servants.

There remained the kings, ministers, high officials, members of formerly powerful families, and miscellaneous nobles. The kings and other nobles were kept under guard in secure but comfortable quarters. Ministers, including those of noble birth, were another matter. There was little need for public demonstration, so most of these were killed quietly. The balance of the privileged classes were banished to Shu. Many of these ended up in camps reserved for labor on future projects that the king was planning. Lu Buwei's former business partner, Li Ziyan, had fled to Wei and assumed a different name. He now found himself in one of these camps.

* * *

General Li Xin was recalled to Xianyang. He brought with him the head of Crown Prince Dan of Yan. King Xi sent his son's head as a peace offering along with a plea that he had no knowledge of the attempt on the Great King's life. Aside from this being rather amusing, no notice was taken, and the search for the king had continued. King Xi was, however, proving to be very elusive. There were rumors that he had escaped to the Khan of the Xiongnu. General Wang Fen was ordered into Yan to continue the mission of General Xin.

King Zheng called a conference in his command center. Li Si, General Meng Yi, and Wei Liao-tzu were present as usual. In addition, the king had summoned General Wang Jian and General Li Xin. The central map had been redrawn. The states of Han, Zhao, and Wei were gone. Yan was shown as a small territory on the Liaodong Peninsula. Another tiny state was identified on the northern border of Zhao centered on the city of Dai. Everything else was labeled "Qin" with the exception of the large state of Chu and the state of Qi. Together Chu and Qi were almost as large as the new Qin.

The king opened the conference with a question: "Which state should come first: Qi or Chu?"

Wei Liao-tzu replied, "Qi is strong both in its army and its government. Its eastern location is far from Xianyang and does not seem to be threatening. Chu, on the other hand, presents a threat to the important Yangtze River basin. Its army is large, but its government is disorganized. It is within our capacity to take the state. Accordingly, the next campaign must focus on Chu."

Li Si added, "I agree with the words of Wei Liao-tzu. In my opinion, the time is good for an attack on this state. The government is in turmoil with a competition between brothers. King Xiong Han ruled for nine years and died of unknown causes. He was succeeded by his brother, Xiong You, who was killed within one year by his brother, Xiong Fuchu. This last brother has been king for only three years, and there is yet another brother named Lord Changpingiun. It is not known what his ambitions might be or what others have planned for him. Considering all this, the attack should be made on Chu."

The king asked, "Is this the judgment of all?" This was met with silence. "Then it will be Chu. How many men will this take?"

General Wang Jian said, "It will take 600,000 men, Your Majesty."

"General Li Xin, how many men do you think will be required?"

"Your Majesty, Chu can be defeated with 200,000 men."

"Then you will have 200,000 men, General Xin. Take General Meng Wu as second in command. Where should the attack strike?"

General Xin replied, "I would recommend an attack from Yangzhai directed at Chen and then taking the area between the Yellow and Huai rivers. From this point, both the capital at Shouchun, and the city of Huaiyang could be taken."

* * *

News arrived from Yong. The Queen Dowager, Lady Zhao, had died. She had apparently taken poison. King Zheng did not mourn her passing. She would be interred next to her two ill-fated children.

*　*　*

Every autumn the king of Chu was expected to make a pilgrimage to Huaiyang, the site of the tomb of Fuxi. Fuxi and his sister, Nuwa, were the first two of the three divine sovereigns of antiquity. They were the only survivors of a great flood that covered the earth. Using divine powers, they created humans from clay. Once created, man needed instruction. This was provided by Fuxi. He taught his subjects to cook, to fish with nets, and to hunt with weapons made of iron. He instituted marriage and offered the first open-air sacrifices to heaven.

Ordinarily the king would spend at least two months in Huaiyang. A comfortable palace was located there, with grand gardens and ponds filled with fish. Li Si advised General Li Xin to assemble a large cavalry force and conduct a lightning raid deep into Chu with the objective of capturing the king during his pilgrimage.

In Shouchun, the Chu General Xiang Yan reviewed reports of spies watching the force buildup in Yangzhai. With the Qin army assembling in summer, and considering the large number of cavalry, it was easy to guess the probable target selected by General Xin. This suited Xiang Yan's plans quite well. He desired the replacement of King Fuchu for a number of reasons, and more than a few officials agreed with him. Now Qin was apparently providing him this service. He did, however, need to be certain. As autumn approached, he "doubled" a few known spies to report that Fuchu would be in Huaiyang as planned and that his security force would be minimal. He ordered that the defensive force at Chen be reduced. There was no need to slow Qin down. Let them have their prisoner while he prepared to deliver a crushing blow.

* * *

In the first month of autumn, the army of General Li Xin and General Meng Wu launched their attack. They reached Chen quickly, and the city surrendered quickly. With this objective met, the cavalry force was dispatched on its mission to Huaiyang while the infantry marched southeast with the Huai River on their right. Scouts and spies searched for the Chu army but found only scattered small groups of battalion size.

General Xiang Yan was concealing his army of 500,000 near Wuxi. As the Qin army moved southeast, the Chu army was slowly moving west along the Yangtze River in multiple columns. They were traveling at night and hiding during the day, using forests for cover.

A few weeks later, the main army of Qin met the cavalry force returning from Huaiyang. In the center of their formation, King Fuchu and several Chu ministers were riding in a wagon. These were sent on to Xianyang with an escort. After the cavalry joined the main body, the army continued along the Huai River.

At Shouchun, General Xiang Yan installed Lord Changpingiun as King of Chu. He then left for his army.

The Qin army crossed the Huai River northwest of Shouchun and set up camp. A force of two Chu divisions advanced on the Qin camp during the night. Just before dawn, they attacked the camps of two corps and succeeded in setting several fires. Dawn broke to confusion in the Qin camp as news of an advancing Chu army was received. The fires were extinguished and the highly disciplined troops gained their order in good time. The army formed its battle line with the river at its back. When the Chu army came into view, it was clearly much larger. General Li Xin had placed the Qin army on "death ground."

All knew what must happen. Sun Tzu had written: "Ground in which the army survives only if it fights with the courage of desperation is called 'death' … In death ground I could make it evident that there is no chance of survival. For it is the nature of soldiers to resist when surrounded, to fight to the death when there is no alternative, and when desperate to follow commands implicitly."

Instead of waiting for the Chu army, the men of Qin attacked furiously. Infantry and cavalry charged together. They killed many, but Xiang Yan's army was simply too large. As the Qin army's losses mounted, General Xin ordered a withdrawal across the river. This caused even more casualties as crossbowmen and archers rained arrows on the men in the water. Once across, the Qin army formed a long line a short distance from the river with weapons at the ready. General Xiang Yan recognized the Qin formation for the trap that it was. If he attempted pursuit, his men would be cut down as they left the river. Even with his larger numbers, victory could be turned into defeat. He ordered the Chu army south.

When the survivors were collected, the Qin army found that it had lost over half its strength.

General Li Xin approached General Meng Wu and said, "I have committed the crime of arrogance, and in that arrogance, I have brought shame to Qin. I give you the command of these men." With that, Li Xin thrust a sword through his stomach and died.

CHAPTER 12

General Meng Wu reached Xianyang with the balance of General Xin's army. He reported to the command center where the king, his army ministers, and General Wang Jian were waiting. King Zheng, clearly angry, looked at General Wu and said, "Who is responsible for this disaster?"

"Your Majesty, I can only repeat the last words of General Xin: 'I have committed the crime of arrogance, and in that arrogance, I have brought shame to Qin.' The general then killed himself."

The king paced the command center in silence with a frown on his face. General Wu remained at attention, waiting for judgment. Finally the king said, "General Jian, do you still believe that you can take Chu with 600,000 men?"

"Considering that the Chu general was able to able to field 500,000 men, I believe more may be necessary."

"How many more men are necessary—one million?"

"No, Your Majesty. One million men would be too hard to support. I would suggest 750,000."

"And how would you use these 750,000 men?"

"I would conduct a more deliberate campaign, starting from Ying and following the Yangtze River. I would time the assault for winter and have a large civil force to secure the army's supply line."

"That means waiting a year."

"Yes, Your Majesty."

"Li Si, General Yi, Wei Liao, give me your opinion."

Wei Liao-tzu answered for all: "General Jian discussed this with us, and we have already advised him. What he has provided meets our concerns."

Turning to General Jian, the king said, "Very good. Now who will you select as your second?"

"With Your Majesty's permission, I would like to name General Meng Wu."

After a considerable pause, the king said, "And you believe General Wu is innocent of this last disaster?"

"Yes Your Majesty. The general did his duty and executed the orders given by General Xin. I know that he will do the same for me."

The king turned to General Meng Wu. "Did you bring back the body of General Xin?"

"Yes, Majesty."

Turning to his chief of staff, the king said, "See that the general is buried with honors."

* * *

The year passed quietly. King Zheng followed his daily routine faithfully. The first duty of the morning was ancestral prayers. These were conducted at the complex of five temples facing the Xin palace terrace. The largest was dedicated to Zhuanxu, the principal ancestor. Inside was a large tablet with the names of all the rulers of Qin. The last name was that of his father.

Zhuanxu's temple was flanked by slightly smaller temples to the other divine kings: the Yellow Emperor, Emperor Ku, Emperor Yao, and Shun. Each was paid a visit. Following this, the king held his meeting with the chancellor and secretary. Then came a modest lunch, followed by a meeting at the command center.

To this were added periodic duties for other sacrifices. South of the complex were the Temple of Heaven and the Temple of Earth. Nearby were the temples of the five seasons: the spring temple, dedicated to the spirit Kau-mang; the summer temple, dedicated to the spirit Ku-yung; the "middle" season, dedicated to the spirit Hau-thu; the autumn temple, dedicated to the spirit Zu-shau; and the winter temple, dedicated to the spirit Hsuan-ming. The Supervisor of Ceremonies ensured that each sacrifice was scheduled properly and the appropriate sacrifice readied.

The late afternoon usually found King Zheng inspecting the construction of the palaces west of Xin. The reproductions followed the contour of the hill overlooking the River Wei. The palaces of Yangzhai and Handan were complete. Yan had warranted two palaces: one for Ji and another for Xiadu. The palace of Daliang was in the early stages of construction. Numerous mansions had also been duplicated. The existing covered walkways were extended to these new structures.

* * *

The Commandant of Guards was very concerned with the king' outings. The assassination attempt by Jing Ke had come too close to success. He had increased the size of the king's escort, but he would prefer that the risk was handled more directly by reducing the number of visits outside the palace complex. It was the same inside. The commandant was thankful that King Zheng did not have a fondness for banquets. These were seldom held. The king did like music, but the performers could be isolated in most cases and thoroughly searched in others.

The commandant had allies. The sage Wei Liao-tzu had advised the king that to maintain his "awesomeness" he needed to be remote. Li Si had similar views. Quoting Lord Shang, he counseled, "If it is desired to do away with clever talkers, then all should control one another by means of the law, and should correct one another by means of mandates. Being unable to do wrong alone, one will not do wrong in the company of others ... What is called intelligence is for nothing to escape the sight, so that the multitude of officials dare not commit crimes nor the people to do wrong. Thus the ruler of men will repose on a rest-couch and listen to the sound of stringed and bamboo instruments, and yet the empire will enjoy order."

In other words, if the law and mandates are fixed and not changed, then rewards and punishments will occur appropriately and nothing will be required of the king. The Taoist advisors echoed this perspective with their calls for the value of non-activity and non-interference.

King Zheng took all this under consideration. He had been badly frightened by the attempted assassination, but that was now forgotten. He saw the prospect of a self-managed government as an opportunity for many other things. Of these, the king desired to make grand tours of his conquests in the same spirit as the emperors of antiquity. For the time being, he placated the Commandant of Guards by delegating the sacrifices to heaven, earth, and the seasons to the Minister of the Royal Family.

* * *

The force General Wang Jian assembled at Ying that autumn was the largest army in history. It rivaled the 650,000 men that Bai Qi commanded at the battle of Changping. There was a total of fifteen corps, each consisting of five divisions of 10,000 men. The cavalry support amounted to two additional corps. The army included twenty-five generals.

When the border was crossed, the advance guard consisted of four corps under the command of General Meng Wu. The left and right guard were two corps each. General Wang Jian and his staff traveled with the main body, which included seven corps. The cavalry corps followed the main body. General Meng Wu placed the equivalent of a full division on horseback and sent them forward in five man squads to scout the country ahead of the army.

The army followed the Yangtze with no opposition. The civil authority was close behind, transforming every community they found.

* * *

General Xiang Yan read the reports with some trepidation. He had lost more men than he cared to admit in his victory over General

Xin. Replacements had been found but the effort had meant the weakening of the southern defensive. The western defense of 100,000 men was retreating before the huge army. He could hope to match General Jian's force with immediate conscription, but there was little chance of gaining a numerical advantage. Even if the numbers could be found, there would be a lack of armor and weapons. The Yangtze plain was very open, leaving little opportunity for ambush. If he was to save Chu, he would need to face the Qin army in an open battle with virtually equal numbers.

*   *   *

At the conflux of the Han and Yangtze Rivers, the Qin army turned northeast toward Shouchun. The Chu army was only slightly larger and was waiting south of the city. General Jian had made several stops to drill his troops. His plan was bold—he intended to repeat Bai Qi's victory at Changping with the same tactic.

The two armies closed to visual range. General Jian deployed first with a line of infantry that extended twelve li (five kilometers). The first rank contained ten corps. The second rank held two corps on each flank and another in the center. The two cavalry corps marched on the flanks and to the rear of the infantry. General Xiang Yan would have preferred to deploy on a shorter line with depth, but he had little choice but to match his opponent.

The armies closed to the beat of drums on both sides. Both sides exchanged archery volleys, followed by a contest between the dagger axe men. After an hour of inconclusive combat, the infantry engaged. After another two hours, the Qin army sounded gongs, and the center third of the line withdrew in what seemed like a panic. It was then that the difference between the two armies became apparent. The Chu army did not have the same discipline as Qin. Their infantry chased the retreating center without waiting for orders. When the retreating men stopped and turned, the Chu army found that it was surrounded on three sides. The cavalry corps now fell on the enemy rear to complete the trap. What followed was a slaughter—300,000 men of Chu died before the remainder threw away their weapons and either fled past the cavalry or waited in shock, hoping to be taken prisoner. General Xiang Yan committed suicide on the battlefield.

General Jian did not wait. He ordered an advance on Shouchun. The army smashed the gates and entered the city. By nightfall the city was in Qin hands, and King Changpingiun was dead.

* * *

The rest of the state of Chu was swept clean of resistance in a matter of months. The civil authorities completed the conquest, this time with civil servants from Wei and Yan. Before long the line of palaces in Xianyang reached seven in number as replicas of both the palaces of Shouchun and Huaiyang were added.

* * *

The following spring, General Wang Fen received information on the location of the elusive King Xi. His army soon found the king and sent him to Xianyang as a prisoner. With the state of Yan completely in Qin hands, the general marched west and destroyed the small state of Dai. Prince Jia, who now called himself King Dai, was captured and also sent to Xianyang. Now only the state Qi remained.

* * *

General Wang Jian sent a letter to King Zheng. In the letter he expressed the thought that the state of Qi could be taken by stratagem. If the forces in Chu were massed on the southern border of Qi, the army of Qi would have to concentrate against them. If his son, General Wang Fen, then attacked from the north, the capital at Linzi could be taken. Without their king and with strong armies to the north and south, the army could very well surrender.

The king and his staff considered the recommendation. It seemed to be sound enough, but there was another problem—the Xiongnu were attacking at the gap in the northern wall between Dai and Ji. General Wang Fen needed to stop this assault. Still, there might be a way to complete General Wang Jian's plan.

The Meng family was, like the Wang family, a source of talented generals. General Meng Wu was the son of General Meng Ao. His son, Meng Yi, was chief of staff. There remained another general that had distinguished himself as a corps commander in a number of campaigns—the elder brother of Meng Yi: General Meng Tian. This man was dispatched with a force of 200,000 troops to Handan where another 100,000 men waited. The three armies of General Jian, Fen, and Tian now included almost all of the Qin military force. The balance was holding defensive positions in the west or scattered in various security assignments.

While General Tian's army was moving east, General Wang Fen completed a rout of the Xiongnu. A security force was left at the border, and his army turned south to join Meng Tian. The forces in Chu massed as planned at Qi's southern border. The Qi army prepared defenses as the two Qin armies crossed the border with the former state of Zhao.

General Wang Fen marched on Linzi while General Meng Tian marched south. The army of Qi was defeated in the same month that Linzi fell. King Jian surrendered.

The descendants of the Yan and Yellow Emperors were now united into a single state.

PART III
Emperor

CHAPTER 13

King Zheng had accomplished much by the age of thirty-nine. Now he needed a new name.

"Insignificant person that I am, I have called troops to punish violence and rebellion. Thanks to the help of the ancestral spirits, these six kings have all acknowledged their guilt, and the world is in profound order. Let the deliberations be held on an imperial title."

A lot of advice was offered. The king decided on a name befitting his accomplishment: Qin Shi Huangdi—First Sovereign Emperor of the Qin Dynasty.

* * *

The state of Qin may have conquered all the remaining states of the black-headed people, but that did not mean it had an empire of substance. Much work needed to be done.

The first order of business was to make some changes to his staff. Minister Wang Wan died of unknown causes, and the Chancellery was given to Li Si. Feng Ji remained as secretary. The position of Grand Commandant was given to General Meng Yi. General Wang Jian was granted his retirement. General Wang Fen was named chief of staff.

Li Si moved to new quarters. He took the *Nine Virtues* with him.

All of Qin Shi Huangdi's ministers and officials had been thinking of the consequences of empire for some time. A trace of doubt did arise with General Li Xin's defeat in Chu, but confidence soon returned. Each function knew much of what was required without instruction from the emperor. Qin Shi Huangdi's commands caused little surprise.

The Grand Commandant was instructed to have the army start tearing down the walls constructed between different states. They were also to collect all weapons found in the empire and send them to Xianyang.

The chancellor and secretary were jointly assigned the duty of transferring Qin's standards to the empire. These would include weights and measures, coinage, and writing characters.

The emperor remembered being examined by Uncle Lu Buwei. The color of his dynasty would be black, for the element of water; its planet would be Mercury; its direction would be north; its number would be six; the preferred body part for sacrifices would be the kidney; and its season would be the same season where many of its victories occurred—winter.

Accordingly, banners and court robes were black in color. The Xin palace was renamed the "Apex Palace," for the North Star. The standard for the length of chariot and wagon axles was set at six feet. The emperor's coach would be drawn by six black horses. And the principle sacrifice of the year would not be in spring but rather in winter.

Xianyang needed to be magnificent. The emperor had moved into the Apex Palace, and the old court building was torn down. The replica of Qi's palace had been completed. This meant that Xianyang could claim to be the only capital with nine palaces. That, however, was not enough. Qin Shi Huangdi ordered the construction of a temple for each of the 360 stars, and another five temples for the planets. These were located on the south bank of the Wei River. He planned to erect giant statues cast from the weapons being collected in the states in the courtyard of the Apex temple. As part of this decision, he provided his Supervisors of Ceremonies a second decision on his burial. The outer coffin would be bronze cast from enemy weapons.

The administration of the empire had already been determined. A map of the new provinces was started soon after the fall of Zhao. It was based on very detailed information provided by the Ministry of National Espionage. The twenty million people in the empire were to be divided into thirty-six provinces, each headed by a civil and a military governor. The borders of these new provinces deliberately obscured the boundaries of the previous states. They were not to be the source of entitlement or reward.

"There is not to be a single fiefdom, even of a single foot of territory. My sons and younger brothers will not be kings, nor will successful ministers be feudal lords. There will be none of the disasters of warfare that have occurred in the past."

Finally the emperor decided that it was not too early to start expansion. Grand Commandant General Meng Yi was instructed to begin planning for campaigns to the west, north, and south.

* * *

In the empire's second year, Gao Jianli was discovered. The companion of the would-be assassin, Jing Ke, had been working as a servant in a household in Chu. He had amazed his master with his skill on the lute. The emperor heard of this and summoned the musician for an audience. The man proved that the reports of his skill were well deserved. It was, however, not long before someone recognized him and he was taken to the Commandant of Justice for interrogation. Considering that his sentence was death, the interrogators were limited in the amount of persuasion that could be used. Jianli would have to be sound enough to face the axe in the presence of the emperor. Still, they were convinced that the prisoner did not know the location of the dog butcher or other conspirators.

When it came time for the execution, the emperor relented, wishing to hear more of this music. Gao Jianli's sentence was reduced to blinding, and he was assigned to the court. Over time he was allowed to play in close proximity to the emperor.

This was Jianli's opportunity. He weighted his lute with lead, and after assuming his designated position he rose and struck at Qin Shi Huangdi's head with the instrument. The blow missed. Jianli was seized, and this time the sentence was not mitigated.

The emperor had now experienced two close calls. He was determined that he would keep a safe distance from everyone at court.

* * *

Qin Shi Huangdi started changing his nighttime quarters. A new palace would be chosen each night. His eighty-one concubines and their children were spread between the nine palaces, along with servants, musicians, and the fine works of art taken from each state. While there were security advantages in this practice, the emperor's prime motivation was to spend a relaxing time away from court with a small part of his family. The Commandant of Guards did notice these advantages, and he ordered that each night's location was to be kept secret.

* * *

General Meng Tian was dispatched with a force of 300,000 men to clear the pastureland of the Xiongnu in the Ordos area south of the Yellow River. He pursued the nomads across the river and into the Hetao. Colonists were sent to occupy the new land.

The Khan of the Xiongnu was a man called Tauman, and he sent his warriors to counterattack. General Tian was successful in repelling these attacks, but he realized that more was necessary. With the emperor's approval, the construction of a wall was begun. It would start near the conflux of the Tao and Yellow Rivers, continue north, cross the Yellow River, and proceed through the Hetao area until it met existing walls. The construction would require thousands of workers, enormous quantities of material, and ten years to complete. During this time, General Tian and Tauman Khan would spar with each other.

* * *

Another force of 300,000 men, under the command of General

Zhao Tuo, was sent south. The army was to advance along the Xiang River into Baiyue and establish lands for colonization.

* * *

Qin Shi Huangdi shared a passion with all the black-headed people—the desire for immortality. This desire is, perhaps, universal. The difference in Qin Shi Huangdi's culture was that people thought it was not only possible but that there were persons who had achieved this elusive goal.

Zhuangzi, the respected Taoist philosopher, described one such person: "There is a holy man living on faraway Gushe Mountain, with skin like ice or snow and shy like a young girl. He doesn't eat the five grains, but sucks the wind, drinks the dew, climbs up on the clouds and mist, rides a flying dragon, and wanders beyond the four seas. By concentrating his spirit, he can protect creatures from sickness and plague and make the harvest plentiful.

"Men such as this are above the expectations of mortals. This man, with his virtue, is about to embrace 10,000 things and roll them into one. Though the age calls for reform, why should he wear himself out over the affairs of the world? There is nothing that can harm this man. From his dust and leavings alone you could mold a Yao or a Shun! Why should he consent to bother about mere things?"

The emperors of previous dynasties shared this passion. The imperial symbol of the moon featured an image of the "jade rabbit." with a mortar and pestle pounding herbs to make an elixir of immortality. The emperors had made a point of meeting and seeking advice from everyone over a hundred years old on their inspection tours.

The Taoists were one of many groups that sought ways to extend life toward this elusive objective. There were many recommended practices and substances that purported to provide benefit. These ranged from simple things like wine with certain flower petals to exotic and secret elixirs. There were, however, dangers, and more than one emperor had died from elixirs that often contained lethal compounds—like cinnabar (mercury sulfide).

The Qin Dynasty was the largest in history. This meant that Qin Shi Huangdi had the resources to pursue the goal of immortality as no one else could.

One of the most intriguing current stories was of a man named Anqi Sheng, who was said to be over a thousand years old. He was reported to have visited the island of Zhifu, where a number of people claimed to have met and talked with him. Sheng claimed to be from an island named Penglai in the distant ocean. The island was one of a group of five. The others were named Fangzhang, Yingzhou, Daiyu, and Yuanjiao. These islands appeared to be white in color from the mist that surrounded them. The highest mountain was on Penglai.

There Anqi Sheng lived with eight immortals. These included one woman, He Xiangu, and seven men: Cao Guojiu, Tieguai Li, Lan Caihe, Han Xiang Zi, Zhang Guo Lao, Zhonghi Quan, and their leader, Lu Dongbin. The eight immortals lived in a palace made of gold and silver. There were white tigers on the islands that were considered sacred. The immortals, who wore robes of white, held the circle to be honored as the symbol of heaven.

The immortals had no need or desire to reproduce, and would only allow visitors who were chaste. The islands would be hidden in the mist to all others. There were many wonders in this land, among them a fruit that could cure disease, provide immortality, and raise the dead.

A Taoist alchemist named Xu Fu offered to seek this magical place. He requested a fleet of sixty vessels with 5,000 crew members and 3,000 boys and girls of physical and mental purity. The emperor approved the request and ordered the fleet to be built.

* * *

There was one final requirement for the establishment of the empire: Qin Shi Huangdi needed to perform the feng sacrifice to heaven and the shan sacrifice to earth. These could only be completed on Mount Tai in eastern Qi.

Mount Tai was the foremost of the five sacred mountains. It was associated with sunrise, birth, and renewal. It was the most important ceremonial center in the land. The feng sacrifice was properly performed at its summit. The shan sacrifice was normally performed at its base. Qin Shi Huangdi intended to complete these sacrifices as part of a grand tour of the empire.

The emperor left Xianyang with a large retinue of servants and Confucian advisors. His guard consisted of a regiment organized exactly like the miniature one that he and Zhu Di had set up in the training center. It was under the formal command of the Commandant of Guards but included a veteran corps commander that shared actual authority. Every man in this regiment was a soldier with experience. The competition had been intense for these few prestigious positions, and only the best made the final selection.

The convoy included two identical covered coaches, each drawn by six black horses. The emperor would travel in one of these while the other served as a decoy.

The emperor made a stop at Mount Zouyi, where he set up a stone tablet and added more scholars with knowledge of the sacrifices. The practice of these mysteries was a closely guarded secret that was never written down. Qin Shi Huangdi was provided the details of the sacrifice itself, then listened to a long list of rules that became more and more bizarre and difficult to adopt. He recalled one of the Queen Dowager's lessons and rebuked the Confucians: "Your master said, 'But while the important rules are 300, and the smaller rules 3,000, the result to which they all lead is one and the same. No one can enter an apartment but by the door.' Now I intend to walk through the door and perform this duty."

With that the scholars were dismissed, the roadway was opened for carriages, and the emperor ascended the southern face and reached the summit. Qin Shi Huangdi performed the feng sacrifice before a huge pile of burning wood. He then set up a stone tablet that read: "When the Sovereign Emperor came to the throne, he created regulations and made the laws intelligent, and his subjects cherished his instructions.

"In the twenty-sixth year of his rule, he for the first time unified all under heaven, and there were none who did not submit.

"In person he made tours of the black-headed people in distant places, climbed this Mount Tai, and gazed all around at the eastern limits.

"His servants, who were in attendance, concentrated on following his footsteps, looked upon his deeds as the foundation and source of their own conduct, and reverently celebrated his achievements and virtue.

"As the way of good government circulates, all creation obtains its proper place, and everything has its laws and patterns.

"His great righteousness shines forth with its blessings, to be handed down to later generations, and they are to receive it with compliance and not make changes in it.

"The Sovereign Emperor is personally sage, and has brought peace to all under heaven, and has been tireless in government.

"Rising early and retiring late, he has instituted long-lasting benefits, and has brought especial glory to instructions and precepts.

"His maxims and rules spread all around, and far and near everything has been properly organized, and everyone receives the benefits of his sagely ambitions.

"Noble and base have been divided off and made clear, and men and women conform in accordance with propriety, and carefully fulfill their duties.

"Private and public are made manifest and distinguished, and nothing is not pure and clean, for the benefit of our heirs and successors.

"His influence will last to all eternity, and the degrees he bequeaths will be revered, and his grave admonitions will be inherited forever."

The emperor descended on the northern face of Mount Tai and performed the shan sacrifice at Liangfu.

CHAPTER 14

The emperor left Mount Tai and traveled to Mount Cheng. There he inspected the mountain, sacrificed to the Sovereign Spirit of the Sun, and set up a tablet. Next he went to the island of Zhifu and climbed the mountain. Sacrifice was made to the Sovereign Spirit of Yang on this peak. Qin Shi Huangdi was shown the cave used by Anqi Sheng for shelter during his visit. The emperor gazed upon the eastern sea, hoping in vain to see a trace of mist on the horizon. He inquired after other immortals, such as Xianmen, but received no report of a sighting.

From Zhifu the emperor traveled south to Mount Langye, which he also ascended. He placed a tablet and made a sacrifice to the Sovereign Spirit of the Four Seasons. The emperor was very impressed with the beauty of the area and ordered a renovation of existing royal structures and the construction of a terrace. Some 30,000 families were moved to the mountain to perform this labor and were given twelve years exemption from taxes. The emperor remained at Mount Langye for three months before resuming his tour.

The next objective was Pencheng, where the famous caldrons cast by the Emperor Yu were reported to have been lost in the River Si. The emperor purified himself, offered prayer, then dispatched 1,000 soldiers with swimming skills to search the river bottom. The search lasted for several days, but the caldrons were not found.

Disappointed, Qin Shi Huangdi left Pencheng and traveled southwest toward the Huai River.

* * *

There was one man who had been following news of the emperor's travel with personal interest—Zheng Liang, an aristocrat from Han who had fallen on hard times. His grandfather had served three kings of Han as chancellor. His father had continued the tradition serving two kings, the last of which was King An. At the very moment when Zheng Liang was ready to follow his father's footsteps, the king, state, and Chancellery of Han disappeared to the army of Qin. Now lacking position and resources, he sought revenge.

He found a man in Bolangsha who was remarkably strong. Together they plotted to intercept the emperor and kill him by crushing his carriage with a huge weight. They found out that the emperor was on the road to the sacred mountain of the south, Mount Heng. The road passed near a cliff before it reached the Huai River. The top of the cliff was covered in thick brush that would provide concealment. The two men went to this spot and began practicing with a metal cone that weighed 120 jin (160 lbs). First the distance was determined. The strongman threw the weight and retrieved it until he had demonstrated that the cone could be delivered to the center of the road. Next, Liang marched along the rode at the pace of an armed soldier. They matched the time of fall with the expected speed of the emperor's guard. A stake was driven into the ground to mark the precise time of the throw.

Then they waited.

Eventually the emperor's caravan arrived. They noticed the twin imperial carriages and had an argument over which held their target. The strongman argued that the emperor must surely be in the second carriage. Zheng Liang countered that this was the obvious choice. Thus Qin Shi Huangdi must certainly be in the first carriage.

As the target carriage passed the stake, the strongman stood and threw the cone. It landed precisely. The carriage shattered with the force of an explosion. Zheng Liang and the strongman fled for their lives. They were never caught.

It turned out that the strongman was right. The emperor was riding in the second carriage.

The debris was cleared and the caravan moved on. The Commandant of Guards was badly shaken by the event and sent cavalry on both flanks.

They crossed the River Huai and the emperor reached Mount Heng, the sacred mountain of the south. There Qin Shi Huangdi set up another tablet and sacrificed to the Sovereign Spirit of Yin. In a single journey, the emperor had sacrificed to six of the eight spirits. There remained the spirits of the moon and weapons. He planed to complete the sacrifice to the Sovereign Spirit of the Moon on the sacred mountain of the west—Hua, which was near Xianyang. As for the Sovereign Spirit of Weapons, Qin Shi Huangdi had a special ceremony in mind.

The entire company traveled by boat up the Yangtze River to the shrine of the Lady of the Xing at Mount Xiang. There they encountered a strong wind, which made landing difficult. The emperor asked, "What sort of deity is the Lady of the Xing?"

The scholars replied, "We hear that she was the daughter of Yao and the wife of Shun and is buried here."

The emperor was furious that a woman, even one of ancient honor, should treat him with such disrespect. He ordered the regiment to cut down every tree on the small mountain, thus making it "naked." The great wind stopped.

* * *

The journey continued to the Pass of Wu, stopped at Mount Hua for the sacrifice to the Sovereign Spirit of the Moon, and reached Xianyang. There Qin Shi Huangdi went to the terrace of the Apex Palace to see the twelve massive statues that had been cast from the bronze of weapons collected in all the former states.

The colossi were all made in the image of famous giants. Around these were a host of statues made from the iron in collected weapons. These represented the tribes of Li as led by Chi You and his eighty-one brothers. Each image had the body of a man and the horned head of a bull. Chi You was identified with a bronze head. The figures had four eyes and six arms. In antiquity, each of these arms carried a weapon. Now all 492 hands were empty, symbolizing their defeat by the Yan and Yellow Emperors.

The sacrifice to the Sovereign Spirit of Weapons was usually made at the tomb of Chi You. Qin Shi Huangdi was, however, convinced that this monument to the end of weapons was the proper place for the sacrifice. The Taoist and Confucian scholars devised an appropriate ceremony, which was performed before a large audience. This was followed by a general festival celebrating the empire and the completion of duties to all eight spirits.

It was not, of course, an end to all weapons. The army of the empire still possessed many.

* * *

With the empire founded, Qin Shi Huangdi was ready to make plans for his burial. First was the suit to be worn. This was specified to be made of gold and jade and adorned with pearls. Next, the inner coffin was to be made from the wood of fragrant conifers covered in gold. The coffin's exterior would be engraved with a testimony to his reign. The second coffin would be made of mahogany and carved with the symbols of the eight spirits, three sovereigns, and five kings. The outer coffin had already been specified: bronze from the weapons of the former states.

The tomb itself was to be twenty-five square li. It was to have chambers for treasure and the bodies of all childless concubines. The number of these could not be determined. Tradition held that to realize his Yang, the emperor needed to have relations with concubines with strong Yin. Since a woman's Yin declined with years, new concubines had to be added each year.

The burial room was to have walls of bronze, with heaven depicted on the ceiling and the empire modeled on the floor. Sacred rivers were to be represented with flowing mercury and golden boats. All important mountains were to be modeled. The five sacred mountains would be cast in silver. The ceiling stars would be represented with pearls.

The complex was then to be armed with booby traps and covered with earth to make a new mountain. General Meng Tian would supervise the construction.

* * *

General Meng Tian was a man of exceptional ability. As a general, he had defeated a larger Qi army and was able to defeat multiple attacks by the Xiongnu nomads. As a builder, he had completed a defensive wall in the west and was joining existing walls in the north. He was improving existing roads and adding new ones. General Meng Tian could rightly be called the architect of the empire.

He approached a construction assignment the same way he approached a battle. The objectives were divided among the corps commanders who, in turn, made specific assignments to division commanders. These orders were then executed by regimental commanders using the manpower and resources allocated to them. The objectives were realized regardless of cost—and in both construction and battle, those costs were measured in the lives of men.

There were plenty of men available. The most valuable were the men of the army. In the past, the army drew its men from the peasant farms and allowed them to return after the campaign was finished. This generally happened within the same year. The wars of conquest that formed the empire had lasted ten years. The new army was mostly composed of professional soldiers with little or no farming experience. These men were physically fit, loyal, and skilled. Those who did not possess the highest level of these virtues had already died in battle. More importantly, skilled men easily acquire new skills.

At the other end of the spectrum were the criminals. These demonstrated a wide range of physical traits. Many were weak, but some were incredibly strong. They possessed no loyalty and had no skills. These men often died from their own stupidity. They were accidents waiting to happen, and there was little that could be done about it.

In-between were a host of displaced people, some good, others not. These were treated like all soldiers. If skill was learned and applied, they were advanced. If not, they were assigned, along with most of the criminals, to the simplest tasks, which were often the most physically demanding and dangerous.

At first the labor force had come primarily from the camps in Shu. Later, the former state of Chu was the principle provider. This was because of all the states Chu, was the most chaotic. All the former states had laws, but in Chu the law was administered in such a haphazard manner that it was virtually ignored. Everyone knew that actual crime was seldom investigated. If by chance a person was held accountable for a crime, punishment only occurred if the right official was not paid. On the other hand, invented crime was used as a convenience by those in power, and there was no appeal from these offenses. Office was sought by many, and if obtained usually required nothing. When the laws of Qin were put in place and administered by honest civil servants, the result was resistance that bordered on rebellion. This, in turn, provided labor to the projects of the empire.

Everyone in the labor force was organized in squads of five, where each man was responsible for the other four. These were grouped into platoons, companies, battalions, and regiments. The commanders of these units could be either soldiers or civilians.

Life in the construction camps was hard but fair. The same discipline was applied to everyone. The punishments were no harsher for the criminal than they were for the respected soldier—and rewards, when deserved, were also equally applied. All ate the same food. There were no special guards assigned to criminals or anyone else.

The regulation for the army camp had been written by Wei Liao-tzu: "When the general (or commander) of the army has entered the encampment, he closes the gate and has the streets cleared. Anyone who dares to travel through them will be executed. Anyone who dares to talk in a loud voice will be executed. Those who do not follow orders will be executed."

And further: "If someone who is not a member of one hundred enters (the company camp), then the commander should execute him. If he fails to execute him, he will share the offense with him. Along the roads crisscrossing the encampment, set up administrative posts every 120 paces. Measure the men and the terrain. The road posts should be within sight of each other. Prohibit crossing over the roads and clear them. If a soldier does not have a tally or token issued by a general or other commanding officer, he cannot pass through. Wood gatherers, fodder seekers, and animal herders all form and move in squads of five. If they are not moving in squads of five, they cannot cross through. If an officer does not have a token, if the soldiers are not in squads of five, the guards at the crossing gates should execute them. If anyone oversteps the demarcation lines, execute them."

When General Meng Tian received the command to work on the

emperor's tomb, it was accepted as yet another battle to be won. A corps commander was given the mission. Soon hundreds of thousands were attacking the terrain of what was to become a new mountain. The other "battles" continued without interruption.

CHAPTER 15

In the thirty-first year of the king's reign and the sixth year of the empire, General Zhao Tuo returned with two-thirds of his force and no lasting achievements. The southward campaign had been defeated by illness, hunger, and jungle warfare. The army was left in Ying, and General Tuo traveled alone to the capital. He was extremely brave, and he stood in the command center and laid the blame for his failure on the Army Command. The only other people present were Grand Commandant Meng Yi and Chief of Staff Wang Fen, and these two men were the Army Command.

"Commandant Meng Yi, I have followed the emperor's orders to the best of my ability, but I have lost 100,000 men because the Army did not support me. The men I led have fought bravely for five years, only to die from hunger and lack of medicine. The supplies I received were meager and replacements were none. Neither my men nor I deserve punishment for this failure."

Meng Yi replied, "General Zhao Tuo, your report has been received. You may now leave. We will consider your words."

General Tuo left and the commandant was left alone with his chief of staff. Meng Yi spoke: "He is, of course, quite right."

Wang Fen spoke: "I did try to get him supplies, but the task was very hard. The overland route is long, through extremely difficult terrain. We tried to supply the army using the Lijang River, but everything had to be hauled across mountains to get there."

"The emperor will not be pleased. This could cost all three of us. Has Shi Lu finished his survey?"

"Yes. He has also completed the planning."

"This may be our only hope. We need to present this project with the news of failure."

* * *

Qin Shi Huangdi learned that the Winter Sacrifice, now called "la," had been called "Felicitous and Equable" in the Shang Dynasty. As this was the new start of the year, he changed its title to reflect its higher status. To celebrate the change, the emperor decreed that every village in the land receive six piculs of grain, worth 10,000 coins, and two sheep.

After the order was issued, he received a request for his presence at the command center.

On entering the command center, he found four men waiting. He expected two of them. It was a surprise to see General Tuo. The Grand Commandant did not hesitate to deliver the bad news. "Sovereign, I regret to report that General Tuo has been unable to execute your command and has been forced to return after losing 100,000 men to disease, hunger, and combat. The reason for this failure lies in our difficulty in supplying his army."

Meng Yi paused as he watched the emperor's face. Qin Shi Huangdi's face reddened in anger. Before there was an outburst, he motioned Shi Lu forward. He then continued: "Sovereign, allow me to present the architect, Shi Lu. He has developed a solution to this problem."

Shi Lu unrolled a map and said, "Your Majesty, mountainous terrain and restricted access to waterways are to blame for the difficulty in delivering supplies. It is possible to solve this with a canal."

The emperor walked forward to examine the map. Shi Lu pointed to a location and continued: "Here are the headwaters of the Xiang River, which flows north into the Yangtze River. Seventy-five li to the west are the headwaters of the Lijang River, which flows south. This river is small, but it empties into the Gui River, which flows to the Xi Jiang River. This last river joins the Pearl River and enters the sea deep into the territory of the Baiyue. Now if a canal is dug between these two headwaters, the Lijang River can serve as both an invasion and supply route for the army. Once it is built, it can also be used as a trade route to unite the empire."

Qin Shi Huangdi said, "How difficult a task is this?"

Shi Lu answered, "It will be a challenge, Your Majesty. There is a significant difference in elevation between the two rivers. By my calculations it will require thirty-six locks and the removal of a great deal of rock. The map shows the best route to take advantage of the terrain."

"This is to be done immediately. General Tuo, where is your army?"

"In Ying, Majesty."

"General Yi, see that his losses are replaced. Summon Li Si." While they waited, the emperor inspected the map on the table and asked for more maps of the Baiyue territory.

When Li Si arrived, the emperor motioned him over to the map table. "Chancellor Si, General Zhao Tuo will be digging a canal to link the Xiang and Lijang Rivers. This canal will be seventy-five li in length and will require locks. I want you to find every merchant, criminal, and idle talker in the east for this work. Conscript peasants as necessary. There are to be no less than 500,000 able men to assist in the completion of this project. The canal must be completed as soon as possible."

Li Si offered a suggestion. "Sovereign, there are many peasants who feel their lands are too small. These would be very willing to bring their entire families south to dig the canal for the promise of land in any new territory."

"Then do that. There will be an exemption from taxes for ten years."

Turning to General Tuo, the emperor said, "General, study the methods of General Meng Tian. Your soldiers are to work with the people, not watch them."

* * *

In the same year that the great canal was started, Qin Shi Huangdi's last living ancestor died—his grandmother, Lady Xia. She was ninety years old. Lady Xia had lived her life apart for many years, first as an exile in Handan, and then in self-exile in Shu. She desired to continue this in death and to be buried apart where "on the east I shall gaze toward my son and on the west I shall gaze toward my husband." The tomb was built at Du in accordance with her wishes.

The emperor left Xianyang with his regiment and two imperial coaches for Shu. There he placed his grandmother in her double coffin on an imperial carriage for the journey to Du. Lady Xia's thirteen servants were brought along.

When the tomb was finished, the lady was interred along with the bodies of her servants. The imperial carriage with its six horses, four chariots from the regiment, and a large collection of burial goods and treasure were added. A temple to her spirit was constructed over the tomb.

* * *

Qin Shi Huangdi conducted a tour of the north. In doing this he was following the example of ancient emperors. These sovereigns started their inspection tours in the east, traveled to the south, then went west, and finally north. For this journey, the emperor used the same regiment of guards as before. For advice, a group of Confucian scholars was assigned. They were led by a scholar from Yan called Master Lu.

The tour focused on the northern wall being reinforced by General Tian. A stop was made at the sacred mountain of the north—Heng. A tablet was erected and sacrifice offered to the spirit of the mountain. The tour then continued to the former state of Yan. The Liaodong Peninsula was visited, and then the caravan moved southwest to Xiadu.

While in Xiadu, the emperor heard of a man from Qi whose father had spent time with Master Cou You during the time of Wei and Xuan. Master Cou was said to have knowledge of the "Five

Powers" and was the teacher of immortals. Master Lu was instructed to bring this man to Xiadu. The emperor occupied the Yan palace and waited.

* * *

Master Lu and the man he sought reached the emperor in the middle of the day. Qin Shi Huangdi went to the Yan courtroom and took the mat of the former king. Everyone else was dismissed. When Master Lu and his charge entered, the emperor motioned the man from Qi to a mat before him and directed Master Lu to sit along the wall and listen.

The man before him was elderly, perhaps sixty, and small. "What is your name?" he asked.

"Li Huan, Your Majesty"

"I am told that your father knew a person called Master Cou."

"Yes, Majesty, that is true. My father has passed, but he did tell things about Master Cou."

"Then tell me about this Master."

"My father said that he arrived from the eastern sea in an unusual boat."

The emperor's eyes widened and he leaned forward to ask, "Did he arrive from an island?"

"I don't think so, Majesty. Father said he described his homeland as being a large country filled with many teachers and even more students, and yet these were a small number in the population. The country was to the south. Father also said that he was quite different in appearance. He had darker skin and a long nose."

"And how did he come by the name 'Cou You'?"

"He adopted the name of the fishing village where he landed. This village was called 'Cou.' To my knowledge, no one knows his given name."

"Was Master Cou immortal?"

"I don't know, Majesty. He did not die in this land. It is my understanding that he taught for ten years, then left in a boat like the one that carried him here. My father did, however, say that Master Cou had magical powers."

"What powers were these?"

"He had what is called 'celestial hearing.' This allowed him to learn the local dialect in a single day by simply hearing it spoken. He was also able to hear the smallest sound at a great distance. Master Cou also had celestial vision and could easily see the small and the distant with a clarity that no one else possessed. Father said that he was able to know other's minds and was able to exorcise spirits."

"Who taught Master Cou these secrets?"

"My father said that the first person to achieve this state was a man named Gautama, and that this man taught a number of disciples who, in turn, taught others."

"Was your father one of his students?"

"Yes, Majesty."

"And yet your father was mortal."

"Yes, Majesty. Father said that the path was very hard and required intimate knowledge of forty-three qualities. He told me that he found himself lacking in the discipline required."

"Are the Five Powers among these forty-three?"

"Yes, Majesty. They are both faculties and powers, so they comprise ten qualities of the forty-three."

"Describe these powers to me."

"My father described it as a wheel of two spokes, which used complimentary characteristics to frame the mind. These pairs were of the nature of Yin and Yang. There was Faith and Wisdom, Energy and Concentration. At the center was Mindfulness. By developing the faculties through meditation and instruction, one was able to apply the same as powers."

"This sounds like the teaching of Lao Tzu."

"Forgive me, Majesty—my ignorance of religion is large. There does seem to be similarities between other religions and what Master Cou taught. Many speak of 'The Way.' In Master Cou's teaching, The Way is a path between self-indulgence and self-mortification. Father said that it was very different, and I can only accept his word. I do know that the object was to escape the cycle of death and rebirth by reaching a high or divine state of mind."

"And did any of his students accomplish this feat?"

"There were four that I know of."

"And these four are immortal?"

"Yes, Majesty, I believe so, although the term my father used was 'deathlessness.'"

"Who are these four?"

"Song Wuji, Zhengbo Qiao, Chong Shang, and Xianmen Gao—all men of Qi."

"I heard of this Xianmen at Zhifu. Do these men have the power of magic?"

"Yes, Majesty. My father witnessed many rituals and said that they demonstrated the powers of Master Cou."

"Can they make potions and elixirs?"

"Yes, Majesty, although my father never said to what purposes these things were made."

The emperor turned to Master Lu and said, "Master Lu, take four other scholars and search Yan, Qi, and Chu for these men."

"Yes, Majesty."

* * *

The tour continued on to the central sacred mountain—Song. There the emperor sacrificed to the Three Pure Ones and offered prayer for the mission of Xu Shi. They then returned to the capital.

At Xianyang, the emperor summoned his eldest son, Ying Fusu. When the young man appeared, his father spoke: "Fusu, I have returned from a tour of the north. General Meng Tian has accomplished much in his important work repairing and extending the wall between us and the Xiongnu. I wish you to learn from this man. I am, therefore, sending you to him. You will serve as his inspector."

* * *

Qin Shi Huangdi held a banquet for the seventy Confucian scholars at court. The Chief Administrator of the scholars, Zhou Qingchen, rose to deliver a speech.

"At another time, Qin territory did not exceed 1,000 li, but now thanks to Your Majesty's divine power and sagacity, the area within the seas has been restored to order and the barbarian tribes driven off. Wherever the sun and moon shine, everyone offers his submission. Feudal states have been made into provinces and districts, individuals are content and pleased with themselves, and there is no worry about war and conflict, and this will be handed down for 10,000 generations. Since high antiquity, Your Majesty's authority and virtue have not been matched."

This was followed by a speech by scholar from Qi named Chunyu Yue.

"Your servant has heard that the reason the Shang and Zhou reigned for more then 1,000 years was because they enfeoffed their sons and younger brothers and successful officials to provide branches and supports for themselves. Now although Your Majesty possesses all within the seas, your sons and younger brothers are private individuals. That an enterprise can survive for long if it is not modeled on antiquity is not anything I have heard about. Now Qingchen is flattering you to your face so as to aggravate Your Majesty's mistakes. This is not the behavior of a loyal subject."

Qin Shi Huangdi listened to all this in silence. He was becoming very tired of these scholars. He retired to the conference room and summoned Li Si and Feng Ji. When the Chancellor and Secretary arrived he repeated the words of Chunyu Yue and asked for comments.

Li Si knew his sovereign well. The emperor was not looking for a rebuttal of Chunyu Yue. He was quite capable of this on his own. He had set the policy of non-enfeoffment, and for sound reasons. The Confucians were irritating and kept repeating the same arguments. It was time to silence them. What Qin Shi Huangdi was looking for was an eloquent statement to that effect.

He gathered his thoughts and began: "The Five Emperors did

not repeat each other, and the Three Dynasties did not copy each other, yet each enjoyed good government. It is not that they were going against each other, but because times change. Now Your Majesty has created a great enterprise and constructed an achievement that will last for 10,000 generations, which is certainly not something a foolish Confucian would understand. But now all under heaven has been restored to order and the laws and ordinances derive from a single source. The common people at home put their effort into farming and handicrafts, and the public servants study the laws and prohibitions. Now all the scholars do not take the present as a model but study antiquity, and thus they reject the present generation and throw the black-headed people into confusion. As chancellor, your servant, Li Si, speaks out at risk of death: in antiquity, all under heaven was divided and in chaos and nobody could unify it, and it was for this reason that the feudal lords became active together, and in their utterances all spoke of the past to injure the present, and they made a display of empty verbiage in order to throw the truth into confusion. People approved what they had learnt in private in order to reject what their superiors had laid down. Now the Sovereign Emperor has unified and taken possession of all under heaven. You have distinguished white from black and established a single focus of adulation. But those who studied privately collaborate with each other to reject the law and teachings, and when these people hear ordinances promulgated, they criticize them in accordance with their own studies. Indoors they mentally reject them, and outside they make criticisms in the byways. They brag to their sovereign to make a reputation. Disagreement they regard as noble, and they encourage all the lower orders to fabricate slander. If such things are not prohibited, then above the sovereign's power will decline and below factions will form. To prohibit this would be expedient.

"Your servant requests that the records of the historians, apart from those of Qin, should be burnt. Apart from those copies the scholars of broad learning are responsible for in their official capacity, anyone in all under heaven who dares to possess and hide away the songs, the documents, and the sayings of the hundred schools should hand them over to a governor or commandant and they should be indiscriminately burnt. If there is anyone who dares to mention the songs or documents in private conversation, he should be executed. Those who, using the old, reject the new will be wiped out, together with their clans. Officers who see and become aware of such cases but do not report them should be convicted of the same crime with them. If thirty days after the ordinance has been promulgated the books are not burnt, then the culprit should be branded and sent to do forced labor on the walls. There should be exemption for books concerned with medicine, pharmacy, divination by tortoiseshell and milfoil, the sowing of crops, and the planting of trees. If anyone intends to make a study of the laws and ordinances, he should take the law officers as teachers."

Feng Ji said, "All copies in the Imperial Library, regardless of source or content, should be kept for prosperity. Li Si's exemptions should include the *Lushi Chunqiu*. I say this for personal reasons, since I worked on the book and I consider it to be the greatest work produced by the state of Qin."

Li Si replied, "Since I also worked on this book, I must agree. The *Lushi Chunqiu* contains very useful almanacs and agricultural advice. Its principles of government have been implemented. Exemption is proper."

Feng Ji continued: "Then I agree with the chancellor's recommendations."

And so the book burning began.

CHAPTER 16

Master Lu returned from his search for the four immortals. He did not find them. When he reported this failure to Qin Shi Huangdi, he offered this advice: "Your servant and others search for the magic fungus, rare elixirs, and immortals, but we constantly fail to come across them. Something seems to be harming us. One of the arts of magic is that the sovereign should sometimes travel about in secret in order to avoid evil spirits, for if evil spirits are avoided a true being will come. If subjects know where the sovereign dwells, then this is harmful to his spiritual power. A true being enters water but is not made wet, enters fire but is not burnt, traverses clouds and vapors, and lasts as long as heaven and earth. I wish that people were not permitted to know the palace where the Supreme One is staying, for only then may the elixir of everlasting life perhaps be found."

"Master Lu, I fail to follow your thoughts. You seem to say that knowledge of the people and knowledge of evil spirits is the same. The shamans tell me that evil spirits are confined to places. Their knowledge cannot, therefore, be very good. As for the people, I fail to see how their knowledge can affect my spiritual power. Spiritual power can only be affected by one's actions under heaven. I have sacrificed to the five sacred mountains and the eight spirits. I have united the feudal states and placed them in a state of order and benevolence. Three attempts have been made on my life and I survived. This could not be if my spiritual power were lacking. Now when I conduct the duties of Sovereign Emperor, many must know my location. When I conduct my inspection trips, all the black-headed people know where I am. I will not neglect either of these sacred duties, as they will not take away from my spiritual power but rather will augment it. Now when I change my evening residence, it is not for the purpose of hiding. I do this because I have a fondness for solitude and variety. Although the Commandant of Guards attempts to make the location secret, still many will know because of their duties. Proper exorcisms are made at each of these locations, and I have never experienced the slightest disturbance by an evil spirit. If your 'true being' will not come, perhaps you should examine yourself for the reason."

Crestfallen, Master Lu left and sought Master Hou. "Master Hou," he said, "the First Emperor is the sort of person whose heavenly nature is stubborn and self-satisfied. Starting as a feudal lord, he has unified all under heaven, and now that his ambitions have been fulfilled and his desires obeyed, he thinks that since antiquity nobody has matched himself. He only puts his trust in the law officers, and it is they who win his intimacy and favors. Although there are seventy scholars of broad learning, they are there only to make up the number, and he does not take their advice. Now the texts of Confucius are being burnt. Since the Supreme one does not hear about his faults, he grows daily more arrogant, and his subordinates, cringing in terror, practice duplicity in order to win his forbearance. When his greed for authority has reached such a pitch, the elixir of immortality can never be sought for him."

They fled Xianyang.

* * *

When it was discovered that both Master Lu and Master Hou had left, the emperor ordered Imperial Secretary Feng Ji to investigate. Li Si offered the resources of the Commandant of Justice to assist.

The scholars were suffering from two delusions common to advisors: first, the assumption that their sovereign desired correction; and second, that they had been retained because of their superior intellect. From this point of view, failure to follow advice could only happen because of stubbornness and inferior reasoning on the part of the sovereign. From this conclusion, it is a short path to criticism followed by slander followed by sedition. The tragedy was that those on this path felt they were acting from noble motive.

The reality was that Qin Shi Huangdi did not need or ask for correction in the affairs of state. He required advice from the Confucians because the social fabric of the people was based on an extremely complex system of rules, ceremony, and propriety. These could be, and were, separate from decisions of law and administration.

The interrogators found that when a scholar was told that his words were seditious, the reaction was that of shock, followed by an earnest effort to blame others for his error. The list of suspects quickly expanded from the seventy at court to a total of 460. These were buried alive at Xianyang. The Confucians would never forgive Qin Shi Huangdi.

* * *

The canal was finished and was named "Lingqu." General Zhao Tuo immediately restarted his campaign to the south. He was followed by a small nation of expectant colonists. This time there was virtually no resistance, aside from a few river blockades that were easily smashed. The horde burst onto the Pearl River Basin like a flood. Resistance was brushed aside, and the army reached the coast and took the city of Panyu on the Pearl River Delta. The colonists displaced local farmers and began staking out their claims to cleared land.

The first signs of resistance were observed by colonists clearing land. These gangs were attacked from the surrounding brush, and those not fleeing were killed. The attacks increased in frequency and size, particularly in the north. A division was sent to one area and pursued the attackers, only to be ambushed. The unit returned with heavy losses.

General Tuo responded by leaving 100,000 men in the Pearl River Basin and attacking north with the balance of his force. His army conquered the small Yue state of Fuzhou, and the region saw peace for a while.

* * *

In the thirty-fourth year of Qin Shi Huangdi's reign and the ninth year of his empire, the emperor approved plans for the largest and most elegant palace that had ever been conceived. It was to be called "Epang." Construction started on a site south of the Wei River opposite from Xianyang. The project borrowed workers from the emperor's tomb. A covered bridge was constructed across the Wei. It was designed to imitate the heavenly Milky Way.

*　*　*

In the following year, Qin Shi Huangdi began his next inspection trip. His youngest son, Huhai, begged to join him on the tour and was given permission. Li Si also joined the company. Feng Ji remained at Xianyang to administer the government. A search was made for Confucians that understood the error of the 460. Such men were found, and twenty joined the company. Their leader was called Master Mu.

One month later they reached Yunmeng, where the emperor climbed Mount Jiuyi and sacrificed to the Emperor Shun. From there the group sailed down the Yangtze River, inspected Jike and crossed Haizhu, passed Danyang, and reached Qiantang. There Qin Shi Huangdi received word that Xu Shi had returned from his quest for the Islands of the Eight Immortals. By return messenger, the emperor instructed Xu Shi to wait for him at Mount Langye.

At the River Zhe, a storm caused waves that were too high to cross. They turned upriver for twenty li, where they found a good place to cross. The next sacrifice was completed to the great Yu at Mount Kuaiji. A sacrifice was also made to the southern sea and a stone tablet was set up.

The caravan followed the coastline north until reaching Mount Langye. Xu Shi was waiting. He explained: "Sovereign Emperor, the elixirs can be obtained on Penglai, but we are always harassed by huge sharks and so cannot get there. We would like to request that skillful archers go along with us, so that when they see them they will shoot them with repeating crossbows." The emperor selected 300 crossbowmen from his regiment and sent Xu Shi on his way.

Qin Shi Huangdi decided to remain at Mount Langye for a time, as he had done before.

* * *

One afternoon, Qin Shi Huangdi, Ying Huhai, Master Mu, and Li Si were sitting on a porch overlooking the terrace and the beautiful mountainside. The emperor said, "Master Mu, I met a man in Xiadu who told me of Master Cou and the Five Powers. Are you familiar with these?"

"Your Majesty, I am not aware of such powers in the teachings of my master."

"Master Cou called them both faculties and powers. They were arranged as the ends of spokes on a wheel that balance each other. He called them Faith and Wisdom, Energy and Concentration, and at the center, Mindfulness. Master Cou said that if these faculties were developed in the mind, they could become great powers in action."

Master Mu was silent. Li Si was clearly puzzling over this until he suddenly smiled and said, "I finally know the solution to Sun Pin's paradox!"

The emperor turned to Li Si and asked, "What paradox is this?"

"Sovereign, Sun Pin was the former Minister of National Espionage. In his office he had a wall hanging listing the *Nine Virtues*."

The emperor interrupted. "Yes, I know. My father spoke of this wall hanging. Minister Pin told him he was having a hard time reconciling his duties with the words of Sun Tzu: 'He who not sage and wise, humane and just, cannot use secret agents.' He commented that the sage has virtue and the wise desires virtue, and yet his duties required non-virtuous acts."

Li Si continued with some excitement in his voice. "Yes. And now I understand! Master Mu, please list the virtues of your school."

"There are five. These are: Ren—the virtue of benevolence, charity, and humanity; Yi—the virtue of honesty and uprightness; Zhi—the virtue of knowledge; Xin—the virtue of faithfulness and integrity; and Li—the virtue of correct behavior, or propriety, good manners, politeness, ceremony, and worship."

Li Si said, "Yes. Now if you consider this list, they are all actions, not thoughts. Even the word 'knowledge' is not used as a mental capacity but rather is meant in the sense of speaking or teaching."

Master Mu replied, "It could be described that way. The master was describing what all know as the virtue of correct behavior and speech."

"So these actions are right?"

"Yes. All know to these five to be right action."

"Well then, let me quote Master Zhuangzi: 'Suppose you and I have had argument. If you have beaten me instead of my beating you, then are you necessarily right and am I necessarily wrong? If I have beaten you instead of your beating me, then am I necessarily right and you are necessarily wrong? Is one of us right and the other wrong? Are both of us right or are both of us wrong? If you and

I don't know the answer, then other people are bound to be even more in the dark. Whom shall we get to decide what is right? Shall we get someone who agrees with you to decide? But if he already agrees with you, how can he decide fairly? Shall we get someone who agrees with me? But if he already agrees with me, how can he decide? Shall we get someone who disagrees with both of us? But if he already disagrees with both of us, how can he decide? Shall we get someone who agrees with both of us? But if he already agrees with both of us, how can he decide? Obviously, then, neither you nor I nor anyone else can know the answer. Shall we wait for still another person?

"'But waiting for one shifting voice to pass judgment on another is the same as waiting for none of them. Harmonize them all with the Heavenly Equality, leave them to their endless changes, and so live out your years. What do I mean by harmonizing them with the Heavenly Equality? Right is not right, so is not so. If right were really right, it would differ so clearly from not right that there would be no need for argument. If so were really so, it would differ so clearly from not so that there would be no need for argument. Forget the years; forget distinctions. Leap into the boundless and make it your home.'

"Now each of these actions can be seen as wrong to some. Benevolence and charity could be used to achieve other things satisfying base motives. These might be self-ambition and a desire for respect, or even an attempt to keep the poor destitute by providing food but not means. An evil man can be honest and faithful in his iniquitousness. Behaving with propriety or good manners is nothing more than pendanticalness. There is nothing in these many rules to justify either right or wrong."

Turning to the emperor, Li Si continued: "Sovereign, I have spoken to you many times of the damage that is done to the present by holding onto the knowledge of the past and holding that as an example. Now since Master Mu and I disagree on what is right and what is wrong, are we not left with the words of Master Zhuangzi? And can we not say that there is no right action?"

All were silent until Li Si spoke again: "Now the nine virtues are eighteen words set in pairs: liberality and dignity, mildness and firmness, bluntness and respect, aptness and caution, docility and boldness, straightforwardness and gentleness, easy negligence and discrimination, resolution and sincerity, courage and justice.

"This list is very old and is attributed to the period of the five divine kings. As such, I was ready to dismiss its relevance. Still, there was something about it that made me keep it and display it in my various offices. When asked, I described it as an interesting piece of art. Now I know better!

"None of these can be considered action, but they can lead to action. The pairs do not represent opposites, rather they are balanced like the spokes of the wheel of Master Cou. Keeping these pairs in mind prevents any of these from overpowering its complement. What results is correct thinking, not correct action.

"Now when I took the duties of Sun Pin, I did many things: I sent agents with false information in the expectation that they would be killed. I forged documents, I corrupted officials so that I could force them to harm their government. I inflicted torture on suspected agents, and I killed all who attempted to do the same things to Qin. My actions would not be called virtuous or right by

Confucius. And yet I did these things to prevent harm to Qin and to assist Qin in achieving its goal of eliminating war. I considered myself right in doing these things. Was I 'wise, humane and just' in this action? I believe so. Since right or wrong actions are only labels attached from one point of view, there can be no universal condemnation from the actions of correct thinking.

"That is the solution to the paradox."

* * *

The next evening, Qin Shi Huangdi had an unusual dream that remained as a vivid memory on his awakening. He sent for Master Mu.

"Master Wu, I dreamed of having a fight with a sea spirit that had a human form. What meaning can this have?"

"Sovereign, water spirits cannot be seen, but they make themselves into huge fish or water-dragons to lie in wait. Now although the Supreme One has been thorough in his prayers and sacrifices, nevertheless this evil spirit exists, and it is necessary to banish it so that good spirits may be summoned."

The local fishing villages provided nets, spears, and other tackle to catch large fish, and the regiment was supplied with this equipment. The emperor selected a repeating crossbow, and the company went fishing for large fish. From the coast near Mount Langye to Mount Rongcheng, in the north, no large fish were found. When they reached Zhifu, the emperor did see some large fish and shot one.

The caravan followed the coastline west and then north bound for Xiadu in the former state of Yan. On the way, the emperor became very ill. He dispatched a letter to his son Fusu, saying: "Take part in my funeral at Xianyang and see to the burial."

The letter was sealed but not sent. Instead it was kept by the emperor's principal attendant, a eunuch named Zhao Gao. This man was the Director of Palace Coach Houses, and his duties on this tour included bringing meals to the emperor.

When the caravan reached Yan, Qin Shi Huangdi died at a place called Pingtai. He was forty-nine years old.

AFTERWORD

The emperor's death was kept a secret until the company returned to Xianyang. A carriage full of dead fish was used to conceal the smell of his decay. There was no effort to determine the cause of death. The decay during the return trip would have made such an examination at best very difficult. If an examination had been conducted, it would probably have resulted in the same conclusion given to Lady Huayang following the poisoning death of King Xiaowen.

Her words were appropriate in both circumstances: "The physician called it heart failure, and I suppose that was right—his heart was beating before and it wasn't afterward."

His last letter was replaced by this: "In Our travels throughout the Empire We pray and sacrifice to the various spirits of the famous mountains in order to prolong our allotted span. Now for more than a decade Fusu, in association with General Tian, has been in command of an army of several hundred thousand for the purpose of garrisoning the frontier, but he has not been able to be received into our presence, having made an advance. Many officers and soldiers have been wasted without a scrap of success, but he has actually submitted several frankly worded letters libeling what We are doing. Consequently he has not obtained relief from this responsibility so as to return as Crown Prince, and day and night he has felt resentful. Being a son but not behaving in a filial manner, Fusu is to be presented with a sword so that he may dispatch himself. Being stationed outside the capital with Fusu, General Tian behaved incorrectly, for he ought to have been aware of his plotting. Being a subject but showing disloyalty, he is to be presented with death and his troops are to be handed over to Assistant General Wang Li."

The letter was composed by Zhao Gao, and Li Si was coerced into going along for fear of his position. Gao had very high ambition. He wanted Prince Huhai on the throne because he was certain that the young man would be pliable to his influence. He had good reason for this confidence. Zhao Gao was one of those eunuchs that could achieve erection, and he was in a sexual liaison with the young prince.

Meng Tian was suspicious of the letter and urged Fusu to seek confirmation. But the prince was in total shock and committed suicide.

Huhai was made Second Generation Sovereign Emperor, and he made Zhao Gao the Director of Palace Gentlemen. The new emperor finished his father's tomb. Qin Shi Huangdi was laid to rest along with his childless concubines. The booby traps were set. The tomb was sealed with workers inside so that its secrets could not be revealed. Work was continued on the Epang Palace.

Under the advice of Zhao Gao, the empire began to disintegrate.

The emperor isolated himself in a world of lavish spending. Taxes were raised and punishments increased throughout the empire. Many officials were executed. Twelve of his brothers were executed in the marketplace at Xianyang, and another ten were drawn and quartered at Du. The bloodbath would consume General Meng Tian, General Meng Yi, Li Si, and Feng Ji. Zhao Gao had the emperor promote him to chancellor and then forced the emperor to commit suicide himself. His attempts to assume the throne were unsuccessful, and a nephew of Qin Shi Huangdi was placed on the throne. Zhao Gao was killed. It was, however, too late. Rebellions had started in Chu and became widespread. The capital was burned, and the dynasty was no more. It was reported that the library burned for an entire month.

It had taken less than four years to destroy what Qin Shi Huangdi had built.

The Qin Dynasty was replaced by the Han Dynasty, but the empire was considerably smaller. The Xiongnu had a new khan, Modu Chanyu, and his armies retook the Ordos area. In the south, General Zhao Tuo declared independence and assumed the throne of a new kingdom called Nanyue.

Despite its short life, the Qin Dynasty had a profound impact on what would be known as "China" in later years. Its standards, coinage, and writing characters survived, as did its organization of the state and the concept of central control.

BIBLIOGRAPHY

Dawson, Raymond: *The First Emperor*, Selections from the Historical Records by Sima Qian, Oxford University Press, New York, 2007.

Duyvendak, J.J.L., Dr.: *The Book of Lord Shang*, Lawbook Exchange, Ltd., Clark, New Jersey. 2011.

Gernet, Jacques: *Daily Life in China*, Stanford University Press, Stanford, California, 1962.

Griffith, Samuel B.: *Sun Tzu, The Art of War*, Oxford University Press, New York, 1983.

Legge, James: *The Classics of Confucius*, Chandran Prasad and Lexicos Publishing, 2011.

Levathes, Louise: *When China Ruled The Seas*, Oxford University Press, New York, 1994.

Sawyer, Ralph D.: *The Seven Military Classics of Ancient China*, Basic Books, Philadelphia, 2007.

Sellmann, James D.: *Timing and Rulership in Master Lu's Spring and Autumn Annals (Lushi Chunqiu)*, State University of New York.

Albany. 2002.

Watson, Burton: *Zhuangzi Basic Writings*, Columbia University Press, New York, 2003.